T0063171

# Sally Beat the odds

A. PHILL BABCOCK

 www.trafford.com
**North America & international**
toll-free: 1 888 232 4444 (USA & Canada)
fax: 812 355 4082

# CHAPTER 1

This is a normal December evening of eighty degrees, in San Diego. California. The sun is beginning to slide, with ease into the calm and blue Pacific Ocean. A boy and a girl are playing catch on the side driveway of a white two-story house lined with multicolored bougainvilleas. A seventeen year-old boy with dark hair, brown eyes, is playing catch with his sister. She is a tall blond young lady in the eighth grade. She has blue eyes, and a sun tanned body with sun tanned stork-like legs. Sally started playing soft ball when she was only six years old in the first grade.

Cooper's thinking. "Last year, when she was in seventh grade she was great with coordination and Sally was a fighter to win. She is still a fighter. But she hasn't touched her baseball in almost six months. For some reason she's missing some catches she should have caught. Sally was fantastic in the beginning of this year in baseball. This year she was still better than any boy that played on that mixed team."

Cooper is still thinking. "My sister can hardly wait until next spring when the girls can have their own baseball team. Now her bother frowns, somehow, Sally, is not catching the ball like she did during the beginning of this past baseball season. And Golly, for some reason she's not even close to catching some of my throws and she's even using her favorite glove.

All this evening she is having a rather difficult time catching. Her brother keeps telling this blue eye girl. "Come on, sister Sally, it's only been a few months since you received that award for being the outstanding softball player in your age group. You've missed way too many catches tonight." He tells his the blue eyed sister. "I'm not trying to play burn out with you, Sally."

His sister returns with her remark, "Well then throw the ball so I can catch it, Coop."

"Sally. That's all I have been doing this evening is giving you easy tosses."

"No you haven't. You're doing something with that ball trying to trick me."

"No way. Why would I do that. Now here is an easy underhand throw. Try to catch it correctly. As he throws the ball, he exclaims, "It's a "pop up."

Cooper has tossed the ball fairly high, wham. The ball ends up hitting his sister right on her left eye and she lets out a squeal.

"Darn you Geraldo Cooper Portage, I'm going to get a black eye just because of you and I have a group of Christmas parties to attend."

"OK, Sally let's quit and call it a day. You need to get a cold compress on your eye."

"No! Coop. Just throw the ball to me as you've done in the past." Just throw the ball and not try to burn it in. Just throw it as we did before and it's nothing new."

This time her brother tosses the ball as a lob and hits the second grader on the bounce right on her stomach. This throw bends Sally stooped over.

She hollers out. "Gerald Cooper Portage Santana, you did that on purpose.

Cooper smiles and replies. "Sally. You're having trouble seeing the ball. It's getting dark and let's go in.

"No way. Throw me some more balls and just be kind to your little sister."

"No Sally. Let's quit now. It's too dark." As they go up the stairs leading to the kitchen, he drapes his hand around her shoulders. Cooper tells his sister, "Sally you were catching the ball last year a lot better then than now. What's wrong with you? Is it your mitt?"

"Nothing's wrong with me or my mitt. Darn you, it's you throwing the ball. You're doing some tricky things with the ball so I can't catch it." That's not fair in playing tricks with anyone when it's getting dark and especially with your sister."

They walk into the kitchen together. Their mother, Greta, has been working in the kitchen and has heard Sally complain while playing catch on the driveway outside their house and complain about her brother's throwing. She hands her daughter a cold pac for her eye.

"What's the problem with you two outside?

"Nothing," Growls Sally. "Mom," Cooper asks, "Sally isn't catching the balls like she did in the games last year. I think she needs glasses?"

A snarl comes out. "I'm not going to wear glasses and be a 'four eyes' for anyone especially for my brother who can't be nice to me while playing catch."

Greta pats her daughter on her back. "Now, now, this might be the time. Dad was talking to me, two evenings ago, about a new doctor that's in the new building that

Dad's in. "Dad said from what he understands she is one outstanding eye physician."

"So this Tuesday afternoon, you are going to have an eye examination. Also, Mrs. Solari, your home room teacher, called me the other day and suggested I take you to a good eye doctor. She indicated you may need glasses. So we are going Tuesday."

"I don't need glasses, Mom. They make you look horrible and the boys make fun of girls with glasses."

"Sally, I know you won't let the boys ever get ahead of you. We've had enough discussions, in the past, about fighting with the boys. By now, I'm sure, they will not be teasing you.

Greta continues. "Well then Sally, if it's no glasses, we can forget blouses, skirts, and those new jeans that are just coming out. "They would have looked great on you with all the six Christmas parties you've been invited to in the next two weeks."

"That's not fair Mom. "Is Dad having dinner with us tonight?" Asks Cooper.

"I don't think so. He called me earlier and told me he has a meeting about a situation in Singapore that needs his input."

Cooper asks, "When was the last time Dad has come home for dinner with his family?"

Greta shakes her head. "It's been sometime ago. Your has father has been given or accepted more responsibility. His travel is now increasing. "That comes when working for a big company, I guess one might say, "It comes with the territory, as he gets closer to running the whole operation."

Cooper is not letting loose. "You don't like that idea, do you, Mom?" "Well, I'd rather have your father home every night and have dinner with the family instead of coming home after midnight.

Next morning around ten, Greta tells her daughter, "Sally, I made a call and tomorrow early afternoon we are going to your eye examination. Afterwards we are going shopping." "What about Coop, Mom?"

Cooper replies, "I guess I'll still wear my old tight, short, and tighter clothes. So, since I'm not getting new clothes, I'll just wear my school clothes to all the parties I've been invited to."

Sally inquires, "How many, Coop? You going to as many parties as I?"

Greta frowns as she looks at her still growing 17-year-old son.

"Poor Mr. Geraldo Cooper Portage Santana, you know, we have talked about it, so we are going clothes shopping in the morning after Sally's clothes shopping spree. "That is, if it doesn't interfere with all the Christmas parties you have marked all over the calendar in the kitchen."

"None of those parties are dress up types, Mom." Sally chirps in, "Well at least be dressed correctly at our Christmas, Mr. Portage. "Maybe we'll bring you a girl with manners who is well dressed. That will be a change for you, big brother." "Mom. Do something with her mouth while your in the doctor's office, will you?"

"Come on Sally let's get going. Maybe we'll catch Dad at his office."

# CHAPTER 2

Gʀᴇᴛᴀ ᴇᴀsᴇs ʜᴇʀ ᴄᴀʀ into a special reserved parking spot next to her husband's car.

Sally remarks, "Wow. Nice parking Mom." "Well, at least we may see your father as his car is here. We'll take the executive elevator to his office."

Greta fishes out a card from her purse. She slips it into a slot and a elevator door opens.

"Two elevators, Mom? What's the other one for, the customers and the workers?"

"Yeah, I guess so. This one is for executives, the higher ups. Hop in Sally."

"Is Dad a higher up?"

"Most certainly. They are whisked up eleven floors. On an office door there is the company's name.

World Wide Investment Security US Division Julius Portage Santana, President Sally asks, "Mom, why do we have two last names, Portage Santana?"

"Because Portage is his mother's family name. This is an old Mexican, Spanish tradition. Perhaps when you get married you may want to carry Portage in front of your husband's last name."

"Nope, I'm not getting married." "For some reason, most girls, at your age, make the same statement. Let's see if your father has time to see us."

Greta opens an office door and suddenly they are in a huge room with computers and workers with a fantastic view of the San Diego Harbor and Coronado Island.

Sally's eyes are wide open. "Oh my, oh my, I can see forever. What is that big boat I see out there?"

A woman walks up to Sally and Greta. "If I'm not mistaken you must be Mrs. Greta Portage and this lovely blond creature is your daughter Sally?

"I'm Mrs. Mitsu Takahashi your husband's office manager." Sally replies, "We came to see Dad and an eye doctor and then do some Christmas shopping. Mom wouldn't let me wear my jeans and tee shirt. What's that out there I see."

Mitsu quickly replies, "That's our US Navy's largest aircraft carrier named after one of our presidents, The USS Ronald Reagan. It's the largest military ship afloat. Huge isn't it, Sally?"

"Wow. It almost is a big as that island." "More than that, Sally. It has more sailors running this carrier than many towns we have in the United States. Mitsu suggests, I'll see if Mr. Portage is not busy. That's a laugh, he's always busy."

Mitsu returns and announces, "Mr. Portage has a telephone in his ear. He is on one of those long tiresome conference calls with six other men somewhere in the world, and another two lines are waiting.

"He'll be tied up for a long time. What a day, what a week, well, what a year it has been. He is constantly working with no breaks. I don't know how he stands it."

"Try living with him, Mitsu. When he has time, tell him we were here. Well, we are off to see this doctor, uh, where is that card?." Greta is fishing in her purse looking for something.

Mitsu suggests, "It must be Dr. Terri McGill? Her last name is one word with no break in McGill. Something about an old tradition.""That's the name. Thank you, Mitsu."

"Mrs. Portage, Dr. McGill's office is just down the hall way four doors on your left. "From what I understand from, my oldest boy, Robert, and thank heavens, he has just finished his residency and has joined a medical group in Los Angeles; and now he can pay his own way. He wanted to be here but Dr. McGill wasn't interested in any more work.

"Robert told me his medical group, holds Dr. Terri McGill in high esteem. She is the one of the top doctors in her field. She is also a down-to-earth person. I love talking to her when we are both on the elevator.

She is a true farm gal over and over and as honest as they come. You'll love her, Sally."

Down the hallway Greta and Sally walk. Sally is excited. "Gee Mom that's some office Dad has. Do all those people work for Dad?"

"All of them and knowing your father they have to work hard. He expects everyone to follow his work habits."

"Yeah. Just like my homework."

"Not a bad habit to have, Sally. Here's Dr. McGill's office." Walking into Dr. McGill's office was like walking into a large horse ranch tack room. Pictures of horses, cattle, and ranch scenes cover the four walls.

Three long tables hold magazines with western photos of cattle, horses, and numerous magazines of Thoroughbred horses with racing photos. There are no chairs, only three large leather couches line two walls of her waiting room.

On the walls are black and white and a few colored photos of various types of cows with these same two tall rugged individuals standing along side some cows and horses. The two individuals in the photos are dressed in western wear.

Greta is thinking: This doctor is a horsewoman. Far different from any doctor's office I've ever been in. Mitsu said she was highly qualified. Maybe she wears two hats, we'll see.

Now Greta walks to the receptionist cubbyhole and is greeted with, "Hi, I'm Doctor McGill's secretary, Ming-hua, and you must be Mrs. Greta Portage and your daughter is Sally Wilhelmina Portage. Correct?"

Sally quickly asks. "Mom, why do I have that name, Wilhelmina? Sounds like a queens name. Why did you give me that name?"

Ming-hua appears to be of Chinese descent. She is a small petite lady with a large smile. Mitsu looks at Sally and tells her, "That's a lovely name and it usually means royalty and you must be the princess of the Portage family."

"I don't know that." Sally glances up to her mother.

Ming-hua then she tells Greta. "Mrs. Portage, your husband made the appointment for your daughter's eyes. We need these two papers filled out and the doctor will see you very soon."

The forms took a few minutes so Greta and Sally wait. Sally is turning pages in a horse magazine. "Mom, can we have a horse sometime."

"Some time. Hmmm. where will we put the horse? Your room or Cooper's room?"

Just then a large tall lady of fifty something years enters the waiting room, she extends her right hand. "Good afternoon I'm Terri McGill. Your husband made an eye appointment with me regarding your daughter, Sally. No one is here in my waiting room so can we chat for a minute or two?"

Greta is surprised at the friendly greeting. "Yes. I'm Jude's wife and this is our daughter Sally now thirteen and going on eighteen years of age."

"Well, Sally." Dr. Mc Gill turns her chair to face Sally. "You are certainly dressed up this afternoon. Do I suspect you two are going shopping later on?"

"Yes Miss or Doctor McGill, was that name right?" Asks Sally. "You got it. Sally, can you tell me, if you know, why you and your mother are here this afternoon?"

Sally takes a deep breath, then gives a quick look at her mother. Sally then replies. "The other evening my brother and I were playing catch and that's base ball. and for some reason I wasn't able to catch many of the balls he threw at me.

"Excuse me, Doctor. It seemed he was throwing balls at me I couldn't catch or see that well. Even when he lobed them I had trouble seeing them coming at certain angles to catch them."

Dr. McGill turns to Greta "Anything to add, Mrs. Portage?" "Yes. Sally, is thirteen year's old. She has been an all star baseball player, from the second grade to this year in the eighth grade.

"Toward the end of her past baseball season, before July, she had some catching and hitting problems. They were like a few times, not many. Then there were problems when fielding some easy hit balls or when up to bat missing easy balls with her swing. Her brother noticed it very quickly. In fact in Sally's baseball playing he mentioned from around her fifth grade that Sally should be catching the baseball without so many near errors.

"Then her home room teacher, Mrs. Solaria, called me the end of last week, as school was out, and suggested Sally should have her eyes checked before coming back to school in the beginning of the year. So that's why we are here."

Dr. McGill looks at Sally. "Pitcher or fielder? All girls team?'"

"No Doctor McGill. I'm a pitcher. We still have some of those boys, on our team until next year. I can hardly wait for the 'Kick Off Day' to see them leave."

Dr. McGill chuckles. "Kick Off Day? What does that mean, Sally?"

"That happens, Doctor, next year when we can have our own girls team in high school and we get to kick the four boys off our team."

"That philosophy you have now will only last a couple more years. "Well, I don't blame you Sally now. In my days we girls weren't allowed to play baseball or play in any sports at all.

"Sally. My school thought, we girls, should learn sewing, cooking and table seating. What a drag."

Sally shakes her head and exclaims, "I'm sure glad I'm not in that kind of school."

Now Dr. McGill turns to Greta. "In yours or your husbands family was their any blindness of any type?"

"Not in my family, but I believe one in Jude's family, he mentioned it once or twice. It seems he had a older aunt that was blind, but not at birth, but it came on later around when she was, I think in her teens, as I was told. Jude left Mexico as a child and his family lost track of that part of their family. Something about a revolution or one of the many uprising in various areas of Mexico or something like that. That was years ago."

Dr. McGill smiles. "Well we have something to start on. Let's go into my room and I'll check your eyes Sally. No pain just a lot of funny looking instruments. "I'll make a deal with you, Sally. After we are through I'll let you look into your mothers eyes with some of the same instruments I used on your eyes. There's no pain, just sit and be still. Let's go ladies."

One hour later, Dr. McGill calls in Ming-hua. "Ming how would like to take this gorgeous young lady out for an ice cream Sunday or soda or whatever she wants. I have a few things to go over with her mother. It's dry stuff and not very interesting for an athletic girl like Sally. About an hour should do. Dig some money out of that petty cash box."

Ming-hua replies, "Call me Ming, Sally. I need a break. All day I've dreaming of a hot fudge sundae with lots of whipped cream and a cherry. What's your favorite, Sally?"

Sally looks at her mother then back to Ming. "A Dusty Road Hot Fudge Sundae, OK mom?"

"I think your brother has been spoiling you. Sure honey. Remember your manners."

For a minute or two, Greta and Dr. McGill sat without talking. Finally Greta asks, "OK Dr. McGill, your opinion. I have a feeling I'm not going to like it."

"Close. We had better become friends on first name basis as we are going to spend a lot of time together."

Greta eyes begin to water. In a shaky voice she asks, "From your suggestion I'm thinking I have a big problem concerning Sally." Greta wipes her eyes and blows her nose.

Dr. McGill answers, "You are absolutely right, except, you and I are in this together."

Long pause, finally Dr. McGill continues, "Greta, look around this room and you'll see a whole bunch of diplomas going up to Doctorates from psychology to medicine all stuck on the walls. I loved my studies, my classes, until I became a specialist in Retinopathy of Prematurity."

"What's it all mean, Doctor, uh, Terri?" Dr. McGill hands Greta a tissue for her eyes. Then she hands her a whole box of tissues, saying, "You'll be needing these."

Terri comes right out, "Greta your child is going blind," Now a long pause. "And there is not a solitary or bunch of things we can to do about it, but only in medicine wise. Forget the medicines completely."

"Terri. It's those genes. Those damn genes. Its not going to happen right now. But it will slowly happen to Sally. It's going to take years, but it will be in time. Maybe, it will be ten or more years before she is completely blind. That we cannot tell. Remember what I'm saying. There are no medicines, no religions, and no statues, no praying, no search for miracles. But only your help and your families help.

"I want you to start right now and this includes your family, father and son. Is there any one else in your two families close by, as we are starting today?"

With a shaky voice, Greta asks, "Exactly now Terri, like today?" "Greta, from what little you have told me about Sally's brother, Cooper, you are ahead of the problems most parents face. You and your family now must plan for the time she goes blind. I can't sugar this problem up with maybes."

"You mean, what your saying there, is absolutely no cure, no medicine, nothing that will stop her blindness or slow it down?

"Exactly nothing, except family assistance and not to treat Sally as having a rare disease or an invalid. I'm serious. I want your family to prepare her for her complete loss of sight when she older. There is a slight change of the subject: Was there a doctor present when Sally was born?"

"No. We were visiting Jude's cousins living on a ranch in some far off place in Colorado. It seemed a hundred miles from the nearest hospital.

"I knew Sally was on her way but not that soon. She came at least two to three weeks earlier.

"So Jude with his two cousins and their mother handled the birth of Sally. Then there was a sudden shift in the weather with a late winter storm, telephone wires were down, the road impassable; and, well, there we were, out in the plains of Colorado marooned."

"Did any doctor check Sally out after you escaped to a town?""Oh, about a week or ten days later. There wasn't much looking.

He said everything looked good to him, except he thought she was a little small." That was the only doctor Sally as seen except for shots."

"Was Sally small as you told me that she may have been premature. Correct?"

"She was a small baby. I guess she was premature as to my count. Of course when the young doctor saw Sally 3 or 4 weeks had passed."

Dr.McGill continues. "I'm not holding this against you, Greta, but there might have been a slight chance, if a trained ophthalmologist saw Sally after her birth. But you would need a careful examination from a doctor, similar to my training and we are not country doctors."

"Thirteen years ago where you were, well there was a mighty slight chance for an intervention. You would have to have a modern doctor that may have caught this problem in the every early stages.

"Even today the chance exists. For you there's no blame and that was too many years ago.

"Right now, Greta, we are going, this includes you, Sally, brother Cooper, and Jude, as well as me. Now we are all in this situation together."

"Greta, I'm telling you, we are going to have the best equipped visually impaired young lady in a few short years to be a poster child for blindness. That's starting right now."

"Well, Doctor, I mean, Terri, I can speak for the family we are ready." "Good. How are Sally grades?" "Straight A's. There is never enough work in school to keep her busy.

So we have reading projects for her at home."

"What about Cooper's grades." "Again, straight A's." "I gather, from Sally's conversation that she and her brother are very close?"

"Together, Terri, they are inseparable. He is in advanced classes. Jude and I, held Cooper from jumping grades. We did not want him graduating from high school at the age of fourteen or fifteen. We are doing our best to keep him normal."

Dr. Terri McGill walks over to a large window and appears to look off into the US Naval base and the USS Ronald Reagan birthed next to Coronado Island.

She turns around and looks at Greta. "I wish many times my folks had that idea. I graduated from a four year college at nineteen. Too young for everything I wanted to do."

"So I hid out in the libraries and became a scholar. Never went to a dance, never had a real male friend or even a date and darn few girl friends. So I locked myself in college libraries.

"Therefore, I have all of those diplomas on the wall for my academic efforts in every advanced class I could take or find. Then my brother never could find a woman that could accept his intelligence. So he, also, remains single on our ranch up north. Some times having brains works against us more times than with us."

"Terri, I'm married to a man that that can't seem to find people, in his business, he can relate to."

"Greta, I had that feeling, very quick, when I first met your husband.

"Now today we have Sally and we have something good to work on. This is not going to be an easy learning experience for the four of us. You, Jude, Cooper, and me, or I, whatever, we four are going to make Sally a poster child, I'm using that term for ourselves as well.

"Greta, sill dabbing her eyes, mentions, "I'm sure, Terri, this will work for all of us."

"Ugh. Not that easy Greta. Not that easy. This road, we are going to travel on, is littered with divorces. Facts and figures don't lie.

"I've been bumping into this divorce factor for too many years. In the beginning, with all my training I thought I could beat it. That's where my other diplomas of come in to this situation and you can bet on it, the wife or the husband will split. Mostly the husband. Why? Perhaps pressure from work to home.

"The wife stays home and the husband is saddled with one huge project. Not money wise but parent wise. If they are both working some one leaves early. "If the wife is usually the breadwinner then the wife is the splitter. But it can go the other way as well. I'm going to watch this very carefully and try not let a split happen."

"Normally this eye problem affects boys and seldom girls. Why? We really don't know. But a divorce? We know and that adds to the whole bag of new environments now busting into a family. "Greta let me put it this way. I'll call this, 'The Blind Children Challenge."

"We are going to have, starting now and unknown to Sally: Start Sally learning about ladder climbing, walking on narrow steps, and adult hand to hand physical self protection. Does Sally ski?"

"She and Cooper can ski every run at Mammoth Mountain. Cooper has been taking Sally with him mountaineering and climbing."

"Excellent, Greta. We'll add all these efforts in knowing she will not have to add these lessons when her eye sight leaves her. She'll just continue right along. I think, talking to her, this is the easy part."

"Terri. I didn't think to tell you but Cooper has started taking Sally with him surfing. She loves it."

Dr. Terri McGill continues. "Sally is way ahead of the game. She needs to continue with all those communications. Holding her consciousness and confidence together. I think she has, with these many opportunities and many methods of communication, she is going to surprise us.

"From your stories and hers, please don't pamper or change. However, baseball is out. Try swimming. I'll give you some names. This is very important. Then start having her room neat and clean, that should be her job, to keep her room always exact. Everything should be in it's place. Tough job with eyes for any girl or woman, I think we both understand that rule clearly."

Greta is shaking her head. "Terri, I just sense this as if a bomb as been dropped on my lap ready to explode and I can't do anything about it." "That's close. You have to start sometime soon Greta. I'll be with you. Are you going to start the family conversation, tonight, over the dinner table about Sally's eye exam today?"

"You bet! Right after dinner, Terri, I'll have a family meeting. Shall I tell Sally about her problem?"

"Greta, it's not her problem only but all of ours." "How do I start?"

"Just what I told you. Be truthful." "All right, we'll have a family meeting tonight after dinner." "Good. Here's my unlisted phone number. If you hit a stall, give me a call. Forget that rhyme or sure, call me tomorrow on the results. Don't push. Just talk. Let me add this, Greta. "This problem, medical wise, these affected genes seem to be located in the mitochondria which are the structures in the cells that provide energy to the cells.

"I assure you Sally will go blind. But let us do our part to help Sally make this trip worth while. For her as for the people that she meets as her teen age years are coming very fast.

"Now. one more problem you and Jude face. It's a conversation you and Jude face. Try to keep Sally's sight issues between just you and Jude. I do know Cooper will get involved. I guess he will take a large interest in the physical aspects.

"Don't drag the kids in it. Keep an open mind, more important have a conversation with Jude and you on any matter. Don't be the Lone Ranger. I know Jude has wild hours going into this problem. The conversation between you two is important along with husband and wife intimacy. Yes I know Jude has to travel the world constantly, but don't loose conversation or sex as a husband and wife."

"Terry, I have a mile of problems to overcome." "I know it, Greta. But so has Sally, Cooper, you and Jude. You're the one at home with the problem. Be strong, willing and I'll give all the help I can.

During that time we, you and I, will fight to hold your marriage together. I don't think that problem should be told or discussed with anyone outside you and me. Lets shake on that."

"Terri, how would it be if Saturday you come for dinner, say around 'seven-ish' Maybe we might have a few rough edges to sand down?"

# CHAPTER 3

Six on the dot, Jude Portage enters his house from the driveway entrance to the kitchen.

Sally is busy at the stove. Her back is to the kitchen door. She says to her brother, and not turning around. "Say Coop some man just came from the side door. I think that's the same man that kisses me every night around 1 or 2 in the early morning."

"Interesting. Very interesting." replies Cooper, also not looking at the side kitchen door.

"Could that he the same stranger that always comes into my room and hugs and tells me, 'I love you Coop.'"

Jude is smiling at his two quick needle-pushers. "OK you two. I read you two very clear. Where's your mother?"

Sally answers, "I think, Dad, she's up in the bedroom going over her notes." "Notes? Notes? She hasn't played that piano in years, just kids." "Maybe she is rehearsing for the family meeting we are having tonight. "I'll go up and see her."

"Be quick, Dad. This can be one upset cook if dinner is delayed. Just ask that waiter there. He'll tell you the Portages have a very nasty cook if people don't come to the table when ordered. Just ask the waiter."

"I'll take your warning with the understanding to be down stairs when you order your father's dinner is ready."

Jude takes two stairs at a time and slips into their bedroom without a noise. Greta is checking over her notes with her back to their bedroom door.

Her husband bends over and give's his wife a quick kiss on the back of her neck. Greta is shocked. "I didn't hear you, Jude. My word, how did you find the house in the limited daylight? Usually you are the night visitor."

"So I receive a slight slam from my wife as well. Those two workers in the kitchen have already had their chance to let me know how they feel about my late night returns. Do you suppose you can give your husband a slight kiss?"

"No. I only give out long kisses. Get over here. I need a kiss from the second story person I hardly ever see in the daylight."

From the kitchen comes a holler. "Dinner is now ready or do we take this elegant dinner and go next door where we can get an excellent hot dinner." Jude helps Greta up, saying, "Our cook and waiter sure run a tight ship."

"Maybe, Jude, I'll keep them on the payroll if that is all we need to do to see their father for dinner every night. Not a bad idea, Jude."

"So now your in with the kids" Are you going to tell me what's going on this evening that is so special?"

"No."

"Is it some secret? Anything to do with Sally?" "Just sit in your spot at the head of the table. There are no discussions of this meeting until after dinner. Greta hollers out. "OK you two, ready to serve? We are coming down stairs."

During dinner, the dinner talk was about Christmas parties. Then Jude brings up a new subject. "Say, why don't we take a long weekend and go to Mammoth Mountain skiing. We haven't used our condo all this year. How about having our Christmas in the snow?"

Yells from Sally and Cooper." Cooper mentions, "I was looking at my skis the other day and wondered if I would ever use them for my senior year. My Junior year in Football is over and Soccer is next. Sure wish we could go skiing before any of my coaches find out that I ski."

"Sally replies, "I want to get as much skiing before high school when I have to work real hard in school."

Greta checks her watch. Then asks, "Is everyone ready for the meeting, especially the youngest and the talkative one."

Sally asks, "You talking about me, Mom?" "Especially you, chatter box."

Jude leans back and asks his wife, "Well, how was your day. Like the new setup, I have in the new building? "Sorry I was held up but a big contract is dangling right in front of our noses. Got to go back tonight to wind up the loose ends." Greta pushes away her nearly empty tea cup and answers. "Mister Portage Santana: You are staying here for a while. We will have a family meeting and you're included. A lot depends on how we handle this problem. Wait till the kids get back from the kitchen before we start."

"And my new house rule starts tonight. Family first this evening." Also can't handle this, whatever problem, oneself. It's not my problem but our problem including Sally and Cooper. Finish your coffee. OK you two in the kitchen, come in and sit down and listen to me." Sally and Cooper trade looks in the kitchen. Coopers quietly asks,

"Sally what's up?""Don't know. If you dated I'd worry but you don't date, yet."

"Sally. One of these days." Brother and sister slide in their dinning room seats and wait. Cooper lets out. "Here we are. What's up, Mom?"

Greta eyes the two across the table, then eyes her husband. She takes a deep breath and tells them. "I would really appreciate what I'm going to say to stay in this house. I know it is nearly impossible to keep secrets in a family but this time really try. Do I hear an answer?"

Three mumbling "yeses" come. Looking at her daughter, Greta announces, "Honey your eye examination found a problem. Your brother was the smart one of the family. Sally, you do have a serious problem with your eyes."

Cooper quickly says, "I was right all the time. It's Sally's eyes." Greta shakes her head. "Not like you think, big brother."

"Sally, you have a problem called Retinopathy of Prematurity. Just say ROP. Nothing you did, nothing Dad did, nothing that Cooper did, and nothing I did. It probably came way back in one our family histories.

"There's no cures, no pain, and in ten or so years, you will be blind. With your family and that wonderful doctor you will begin to learn to stay the lovely lady you are now."

There was not a sound from anyone at the table. Sally was the first to ask, "Did Dr. McGill tell you that today while Ming-hua and I went out?"

"That's why you two went for sundaes." "OK. How many days do I have before I become blind? "Sally it's years not days. I'm suggesting we, as a family prepare you, honey, to begin certain courses in school.

"We'll begin with different athletic interests, learn the art of Braille before you need it and learn to use talking books while you can see. And the really tough one is to learn, now, to keep your room neat."

Jude is wiping his eyes. "Are you sure this is a fact, Greta and not a guess?"

"Terri, Dr. Terri McGill, showed me, using one of her instruments, and pointed out Sally's optic nerves.

Sally looks around, tears in her eyes, asks, "What about baseball, Mom?"

"That's out Sally. I talked to Mr. Granger at your school. He's the one that has a junior swimming class. He knows you have already raced in your school swimming class sprint races and won. Mr. Granger has a friend that is now taking over San Diego's 'The Blue Sharks.' Aren't two friends, Beth and Liz on that junior swim team?"

"Yeah. I can or could beat them early this summer in sprints. You mean, Mom, I can swim even when blind?"

"Absolutely. Only when that time comes, you will swim in one of the outside lanes, according to Mr. Granger. He said Coach Rolland, later, will have two whistles of different sounds. One tone will tell you when to turn around and the other tells you if you are getting close to the edge or to your opponent." How does that sound to you?" You mean they will take me on their team if I show up and practice?"

"This is, only if you show up and really practice. You will use a whistle before you will need a whistle."

"Gee, they have really good looking racing suits. Can we check them out next week?"

Jude pats his wife on her back and bends over her, "I think you have this under control, Greta. I have to get back to work. Should be home around twelve. See you in the morning kids."

Its quiet for a moment or two, Cooper then breaks the silence with, "We all can do it. When skiing, we'll have a rope around Sally with one of us telling her where to turn. Or eventually it will be a round pole with two of us, one on each end, guiding Sally. We've seen all this on the slopes before. No problem."

Sally interrupts, "No problem you say. As I understand it, I'm in the middle or tied with one of you behind me. I don't know if I trust any one of you on a ski slope. I'm just a better skier than any one in this family and that will stay true for some years. So don't plan anything too fast for me."

Cooper continues. "We can do it. I can even take Sally out on my board for surfing. She rides while I stand and control it. That is with no great waves."

"Wait a minute Cooper Portage Santana." came the call, again, from Sally. "This eye problem is not going to happen over night. Maybe I'll be in college before I go really go blind. Right Mom?"

Cooper replies, "True, little sister. But don't you want to go now before you have learn how?

Sally looks at her brother. "Huh? I'm just going to be blind then need help. But not for some time. I'm certainly not trying to figure out what you said with your stupid sentences, brother."

Greta looks at her two charges and smiles. She's thinking, this was easier than I thought or are they just playing up to me. Well time will tell. We all have to keep Sally busy and Cooper is going to be a jewel for me. Wait till I phone Terri.

Greta returns and announces, "Dr. Terri McGill will be here tomorrow night for dinner. Cooper, she's a great lady with common sense. "She and her brother own a horse and cattle ranch in Northern California, some place near Fort Jones. She said they have a large cattle drive in the late summer.

"Terri told me they always need people on horses to help. We'll see gang. Now off to bed. Cooper, tomorrow, we are going shopping for some decent clothes. I'm tired of your current dress attire." "Count me in Mom. Can I go with you two?" asks Sally.

Cooper stands an tells the ladies, "My only hope is to get sick tonight. Good Night ladies."

Then he went to each with a good night kiss. He tells his sister, "Love you babe. You know I'll always protect and support you."

Then he stops by his mother. "Mom, our family will be stronger and better from now on." He gives her good night kiss.

Greta grabs her napkin and wipes her eyes. She's thinking, I don't know if the kids are just playing with me or they are on the level.

Greta and Sally stay up for another hour or two talking. "Sally, no one can stop the this from happening. Dr. Terri McGill will be here for dinner Saturday night. You can unload on her any medical questions.

"As of now we will begin to practice, for your future blindness, so when the time comes, in years ahead, you will be completely blind and absolutely prepared anywhere in about five to ten years from now."

Cooper asks, "Is that how long that will be, Mom?" "All Dr McGill told me is we just can't really say now. "It will be ten to fifteen years without any medical help. With the best, and millions of dollars spent for medicine and/or church prayers, it's about the same."

Sally reminds her mother, "Gee that's going to tough. What about the baseball team without me?

"Greta shakes her head. "Forget it. Now it is swimming. We'll have more on that subject tomorrow night when Dr. Terry McGill arrives. Lets head for bed, honey."

Dr. Terri McGill arrives at the Portages house near five PM. Jude also came home early.

Cooper runs out to give Dr McGill a hand. "I'm Cooper, Dr. McGill." Thanks Cooper. At my age I need all the hands I can get. Can you carry that pie straight up, I'll handle the wine."

They start to the house going to the side door to the kitchen. Terri asks Cooper, "How's school?"

"No problems. Finally soccer practice is about to begin." "I thought your mother told me you played football?"

"I did. My third year of football season is over. But all I ever did was kick the ball, did punts, kickoffs, extra points, and field goals. "My coach would not let me play in the game. Something about I was to valuable. It's not fun just to watch the game and not play in it."

"Cooper you have made more points for your team than anyone one player the league."

"Yeah, it's something like that but still I wanted to play."

"Cooper, You were voted the most valuable player in the league again and that was the third time. Some of your kicks were spectacular in length and direction. Young man, If I were your coach I wouldn't let you play either. Just like your quarterback, he only plays offense. You'll never see a quarterback playing defense. Am I right?"

"It sounds as though you watched some of our games, Dr. McGill?" "Every home game I did. I was screaming as loud as any mother of a player. I enjoy high-school football games. My brother was an All American at Duke. But in high school football, any thing can happen in high-school games and they do."

"I'll be sure to listen for you next fall." "Cooper I want to say this to you. I'm impressed with your care of Sally. As she grows older she will need a brother she can count on. Your ages separate you two, but later on they won't. In horsemanship we have a sentence to remember."

"Give them some rein but don't pull back too much or hard or show any blood in their mouth or on their body. "Keep the reins too loose or to tight and they will try to run away."

"What does that all mean, Doctor?" "It means a firm hand but a light hand with the reins whether going straight ahead or on turns. Don't haul your horse around or pull hard back on your reins. Let them go with your weight directing a slow gait or stop or turns. They learn quick and treat Sally the same way. Keep your hands on the reins but let her go within reason. Remember, One hand for the horse and one hand for the rider, that's you."

When Dr. Terri McGill entered the kitchen, she looked at Sally. "Did your mother say anything to you about swimming?"

Thank you. We saw him, Coach Rolland, and he told me he always wanted me on his swimming team but my baseball came first."

"Mom, remember, he told me I can join his swimming team and wear those good looking white and blue swim suits his varsity team uses?"

Greta replies, "That promise was, If you work hard." "What about my eyes?"

"It's all taken care of, Sally." Dr. McGill adds. "Sally, I know Coach Rolland. He's tough on slackers. With you joining his team this will make every girl, on his team, work harder and of course, knowing you, Sally you will work even harder. Everyone wins."

Dinner is over and Jude is off back to the office for more work. Greta stares at the front door now closing. She bites her lip and her eyes water up.

Terry catches Greta's look. "Say gang I have a job for you all in the late summer. How would you three like a two week roundup on our ranch in August before school starts. I need riders."

Sally jumps in with, "You mean we become cowgirls?" "Not exactly Sally. We have boys as well. Each of you will be assigned a horse, rather two horses. We keep changing a horse each day. In the morning You'll feed them, curry them, ride them, then after the work day is over, you'll curry them, feed them, and do this every day.

It is important that you won't have breakfast or dinner until your horses are first fed. That's a cowboy law. I or my brother or Tito Ortiz, our foreman will help you. I'll make cowboys and cowgirls out of you three. Interested?"

Sally is almost jumping out of her chair. Greta is smiling and nodding her head. Cooper is frowning.

Terri asks, "Cooper, is something wrong about my offer? "Well football practice starts two weeks before school starts."

"Coop. Which coach takes care of the special teams?" "Coach Spec Harrison." "I know him. I did some work on his eyes, two years ago, so he doesn't have to wear glasses. I'll talk to him and make sure you'll practice your kicks every morning and evening. I'll call him tomorrow."

"What an offer, Terri." Greta is smiling. She weighs in, "It's been years since I was on a horse and that was when I was growing up back east, riding English style. 1 did some jumping but our saddles were flat and we used reins unlike our western gear, as I remember."

Dr. McGill replies, "Greta, going from English to Western is easier than Western to English. You already have the balance.

"Sure, you'll be sitting slightly different as we have western saddles. We ride the "Vaquero" or California or the Spanish style. We sit straight up, stirrups straight down, with the reins in one hand, and other arm straight down, and no trotting. You'll catch on quick and a lot quicker than the kids.

"Oh, gang, you'll need western boots, levies, cotton shirts and a jacket, and Western hats. Some cowboys use baseball hats but you have to be a good rider to put that across. If your hands are tender, like mine, we'll need light gloves. Dark glasses accepted. And at the ranch we do not have a swimming pool. We have a good size creek which dammed off. It's a nice spot to wash the dust off but very cold water. "Let see, what have I missed. Oh yes, we are up at five to feed our horses. Six for breakfast and Lee Wong, our cook, will have an ample breakfast and be out on our horses at eight and that will be something new for you guys.

"After breakfast we curry and saddle up our horses and then we'll ride off for the day. You pack your own lunch. Lee will have fixings on a table in his kitchen. Just stuff what you want on one of the saddle bags. We'll be back at the ranch around five or six in the evening. Lee will have dinner at seven. Have your horse curried before dinner.

"The California Western horse rule is, 'Have your horse taken care of before you do anything else for your self. There are no questions until your horse work is complete before you eat.

"We have no television as we are cut off from any direct line. We do have radios. Usually there will be five or six other ranches also collecting their cattle. Some of them may stay over for a night or two.

"What cattle we find each day we bring back with us to our ranch and each ranch cuts out their branded cattle. So we may have visitors staying with us, off an on, for a couple of weeks.

"They will have their kids with them so plenty of young cowboys and cowgirls will be around. I said that for you Cooper. Sally I believe there will be three or for girls your age.

"These kids are country smart. They'll teach you two a lot. Usually they will sleep out in our big porch or use their folks horse trailers. With six bedrooms and a large living room plus our porch we can sleep an army. Our own cowhands, three, have their own cabins. Any questions?"

Sally is quick to ask, "If those kids ride horses and we don't know how, then how can we keep up with them sitting on a saddle all day."

"Sally, most of the kids, are in high school or junior high. Two or three families with kids live in town and come home only on weekends. So they will be as sore in their rear ends, same as you guys. Don't worry about it. Oh Sally, if I were you, I wouldn't mention anything about your eyes. You won't really know you have a bad eye problem for many years, If something regarding sight, shows up doing something, just fake it, Sally. Just say, you forgot your glasses."

"Now you, Cooper: You are an all star football player in high school for four years and now off to college with two scholarships. These older kids, especially one, will be very interested in you and of course two or three of the older girls a well. I would think after this summer, every summer from then on you two and your mother will be cow hands and have many new friends.

"How old are some of those ranch girls?" asks Cooper. "I think two or three are freshman in school. Does that answer your question?

"Oh, one is a sophomore or a junior. Her brother is a big boy and treats his sister just like you treat Sally. He keeps an eye on her, constantly."

"I'm not really interested, I just asked a common question, Dr. McGill."

Sally jumps in, "Coop, you're lying your white teeth. The freshman, sophomore, junior and senior class girls would almost do anything to attract your attention.

"When I see one or two of them walking past our home they always ask me, "Sally, how's your brother. Is he dating anyone? What college is he going too?"

"OK, OK, sister. What do you tell them when they ask you, for some reason, that question?"

"What question, Coop?" "Holy smokes. The question about if I'm dating anyone."

"Oh that question. I just tell them my brother only dates me." Raising his voice. "Sally Wilhelmina Portage Santana, just the truth." Demands Cooper.

"Oh, I just tell them he has a list a mile long and that someday he'll use it. Right now he stays home learning to dance. Anyway Brother Cooper, aren't you entering Cal Poly in San Luis Obispo on Football, Soccer, and Academic Scholarships and classes in girl watching who will "None of that. I really tell these girls, "I'm not dating as I haven't found a girl who will go out on a date with me even to an afternoon movie." "How does that sound?"

"Mom, make her tell the truth."

"Honey your sister is pulling your leg. She's just getting back to you and really you deserved it." "When go on your ranch Dr. McGill, I want to be sure I wont be riding next to my sister."

"OK Cooper," says Dr, McGill, "I'll remember that. However, I know a cute freshman or maybe littler older girl that barrel races and enters goat tying contests and wins.

"She is tall, deep blue eyes and as a cowgirl, she walks like a model. Maybe I'll ask her to teach you how to stay on a horse and ride like a cowboy."

"She also has a huge brother, a senior and all conference defensive tackle, and an all conference heavyweight wrestler with a scholarship to UC Berkley. His name is Meredith but goes by Butch. He watches his sister very close. Kinda like you do with Sally.

"I'll introduce you to Meredith when you guys come up to our ranch and become cowgirls and a cowboy."

Cooper stands up and smiling, says to the three ladies, "Whatever. There are two things I'm going to do. One is going to bed and secondly, to become a cowboy. Good night to all and you on the chair, I hope you, funny one, will have some good old nightmares tonight. "Mom, is it tomorrow for new clothes, kinda like Christmas shopping?"

"In the morning, Mr. Portage, shower and touchup your face with your electric razor, then we'll go Christmas shopping.' Greta smiles as Cooper leaves the room.

Sally is still awake. She wants more information on Dr. McGill's ranch. "Well, lets see Sally. Our ranch is about 7000 feet up in the mountains. We are close to being snowbound in the winter. So provisions must be bought in the fall, like canned or frozen foods. Toilet paper, batteries, fuel for our furnace and our ski mobiles.

"We have electric lights but when there is a good snow fall, the electric wires may break. My brother and Tito, our year-around foreman, and his wife, Jessie, will spend the winter fixing up everything used during the spring, summer, and the fall.

"They have added on our house more bedrooms, toilets, closets, and two large garages. This housing is for our fall roundup. Our horses must be fed. And two cows must be milked.

"Our cows and horses will stay in the barns, during winter and after a heavy snow storm will remain in the barns. So the manure is stacked on sleds to we pulled by our snow mobiles and dumped in an isolated area. We try to clean out our horse stalls nearly every day weather permitting."

Sally has taken this information in carefully. "You mean, Dr. McGill, these three people spend all winter alone on a ranch they can't leave due to the snow?"

"That's just about right, Sally." But there are people, who will spend days and weeks walking up hills to ski down. We have seen some skiers at Mammoth ski using touring bindings and skis. "But they ride up the mountain like we do to ski down. And you're saying, Dr. Terry, people come to your ranch to walk up a mountain, in the snow, to ski down to walk up again to ski down to walk up, still packing their skis up again to ski down, and again, and again, and again?"

"Sally," Dr. McGill is laughing. "Honey that is called cross-country skiing. People were doing that type of skiing long before automobiles. They worked, fought wars, lived in the snow. and they survived. Today people are cross country skiing to escape the skiing crowds.

"Also the quietness is very similar as hiking in the mountain and getting away from crowds to enter the quietness of the grandeur of the outdoors.

"Sally, these outdoor people, coming here in the winter, are the same as the people who ride up the mountains to ski down. The also like winter sports with less people to be around. Interesting, isn't it?"

Sally interjects, "I don't think I could live very long with no telephone, no one to play with, not seeing any of my friends, being alone for a long time. No I don't think I could ever do that, now especially with what's going to happen to my eyes."

Greta grabs Sally and sets Sally on her lap. "Young lady, our early ancestors lived that life without the conveniences we have now. The strong intelligent ones, those that prepared for winter, made it through. The weak or lazy, well they just passed away.

"Aren't we lucky living our life without those hardships? Yet, many of them lived a long life facing starvation, sickness, and the unknown. Could we have done the same? Yes, if we lived in their environment?

I'm glad we aren't but in our world people still live and survive in such a hostile environment; yes, even today as we sit in a warm house with electricity and friends. Lucky you say? It's not luck. They have the will to survive like you my dear. They survived and you will because you have the will to survive. Time for bed young lady."

Sally then asks, "With two weeks on the ranch riding horses and taking care of horses, what about clothes, Dr, McGill?"

"Tell you what gang, in May or June we'll stock up in proper attire. It will give you three a chance to break them in and have a few washings. "I have a client in the Otay Lakes area and we'll ride his horses on the summer weekends getting our rear ends ready. In fact I need to get my rump ready, as well."

Then with a kiss and a hug to Terry and Greta, Sally heads off to bed.

Greta waits until she is sure Sally is out of hearing. "With just the normal slow and the explosive conditions of youth, I think and hope Sally walks that thin line from a child, to a teenager, to an adult, carefully."

"Greta, It's a tough situation for parents, with young adults, to keep everything, from head to toe working, and the brain and the muscles in progression, I think that girl is not going to let her vision mess up her life." counsels Terri.

Terri wipes her eyes. "Greta that was a great talk. You and Cooper will be the family of the year with your feeling and judgment with Sally. Now what are we going to do with Jude?"

"I don't know. It will one of three. Either I'll be a wife, a divorcee, or a widow. Something has to go and I don't like my chances in any of the three options. Give me some time to juggle this, I guess this cloud that sits over me and the kids will stay for a while.

I love Jude. He has given us a good life, and wonderful home, money in the bank and great investments. He has the kids college funds set aside until they graduate and find a job. Cooper and Sally do not know what or if their father has set aside money for them.

"Cooper gets a car when he goes off to college. However Coop wants an old pickup. Then there is money set aside in Coopers name for college expenses. The same for Sally. We had to make a change with Sally. It will be taking trains and planes for her."

In the middle of January, Jude came home from work early without being ordered. Cooper is the first to ask, "What happened, Dad, You got fired?"

"Me? No way. Take a better guess than that?" Sally enters "Twenty Questions." "I know. I know. You bought out a bank and you'll be home early every afternoon." Greta is last. "Hmmm. Hopefully you have quit your position." Jude laughs. "One thing is certain. You, my family, just don't like my working hours. I'll tell you after dinner." "Oh come on Dad, that's not fair." Cooper is anxious.

"Listen to me, that's all three of you. As mother did it before, regarding Sally. "Again each of you will be pleasant, be polite and try show me some respect as the only worker in the Portage family. And that silence will remain until after dinner."

"But Dad." came the voice from Sally. "My meeting was of medical importance. We all had to know."

Jude is smiling. "Sally, you could be an attorney the way you can dig into a statement except you fail to understand. All right. I will give you all a clue. Are you three ready?

Three heads bob up and down. "OK, hear it is. "Don't ask me any more questions until dinner is over with. "I love hot dinners on hot plates. Is our cook and waiter ready to serve?"

After dinner, Jude announces, "Let's take a 3 day ski trip to Mammoth Mountain over the Presidents weekend in February. Just the four of us. Do I have any takers?"

Three people respond. "We are ready." Greta is surprised. "Jude, you told me January and February are tight months for you. What happened?" "A crazy thought came into my mind as I was looking over my schedule. I'm going to do a lot of traveling until September. It will be in the papers tomorrow.

You are now looking at the President and the Chief Officer, and Chairman of the board. And I guess what ever else they can think of titles. It's a one man show.

Personally, I have to straighten out the company. After that I leave them. Please keep that under your hats. I can't leave the company until every thing we do is running smooth. I just can't."

Greta is in shock. "You mean you will walk out sometime next year. what are you going to do then?"

"I have been toying with a few items along with two of my associates. I can't go any further with that now.

"So lets get back to skiing. Instead of going through opening and closing our house we'll stay at the hotel and have a great long weekend skiing, if those two young ones will let us ski with them."

Greta is still surprised. "Jude, one year and you are out?" Correct?" "If nothing happens, Yes. I'm so tied to this company that it's going to be hard to exactly know when I can leave. It may be a bit longer, but I'm walking out in one year to three years or four and not a day longer. They know that." Greta shakes her head. "I don't know about that, Jude. I just can't see the company letting you walk away with all your help and knowledge."

Greta continues, "We'll see. So it's a go for skiing. You know something? "Well don't worry about that Greta.

We'll fly up to Mammoth Friday night and come home Monday night. Then we'll have three full days skiing."

"Jude, you can't just do that unless you have an airplane." "There's one more item, Greta. Now being the head man I wiggled a charter airplane for company service. It's Josh Hammerlee, who is one our biggest stock holders.

He has a jet that flies him anywhere he wants to go. So he turned the plane over to us for the weekend. We will even have a Flight Attendant aboard. It's Josh's 18 year old daughter, Jessie or sometimes called Jessie Bell. "I made one rule. If there's questionable weather going or coming, then it's a no-go even with two qualified pilots.

"It's Josh Hammerlee with a 'million' hours flying and his copilot, a retired Air Force senior pilot, Abe Sinclair.

"Also his daughter, Jessie Bell, who has been flying since she was 14, only in jets. She will be the third pilot and Flight Attendant.

"I talked to all three pilots. My rule is that," 'Under no circumstances will we fly under questionable weather even if the airlines are flying.' It's my contract when flying in our own airplane."

Early on Saturday morning the Portages loaded their ski equipment aboard their twelve passenger jet.

"With it came the opulent master compartment. They looked in at the compartment with a single recliner chair. There was a pull down bed, and toilet room made, big enough for a king. The Portage's took the seats instead.

Their flight lasted under an hour. Sally told her friends, at school, "We lifted off climbed up and came down. There was not even an hour used up. I think we spent more time packing and storing our skis and baggage."

Mammoth Mountain skiing grabbed Sally and Cooper. At eight in the morning those two climbed on the gondola to ride to the top of Mammoth Mountain, and ski off on Dave's run.

In the gondola is a 16 year old young lady skier. She asks, "You two going all the way to the top?"

Sally answers, "Yep. My brother and I only ski off the top." "You two certainly don't live here as I've never seen you before.

My name Kitty Johnson. I used to be on Mammoth's race team but got kicked off. They didn't like me horsing around.

So I'm studying to be a Ski Patroller. All I have to do is pass their mountaineering and first aid test this spring. Oh, and turn eighteen."

Sally introduces herself and tells Kitty "I ski with my brother, Cooper. This is our first time up this year."

Kitty asks, "Are you two familiar with the runs off the top?" Cooper mumbles out, "Somewhat. We'll follow you, Kitty." Arriving on top of Mammoth, the three step in their skis, check their bindings, do a couple of stretches then Sally disappears over the crest headed straight down.

Kitty gasps, "Holy cow, I don't think we can catch her. Your sister is nuts."

Cooper answers, "Let's catch her before we lose her." And Cooper shoves off using three skating pushes then moves off and is heading straight down, then goes into a series of hops.

Three young skiers never stopped until they reached the midway point. With their skis off, riding in the gondola, the three are riding back up to the top.

Kitty exclaims, "You guys are here on your first day this year and skiing like that?"

"Yeah," answers Sally. "Good run. Kitty, my brother and I ski fast in the morning, then in the afternoon we just cruise around with our folks. Want to join us today skiing?"

"You two guys would make really good down hill racers. Sally answers, "Nope. I can't see the poles outlining the runs. Also it's no fun doing the same run all the time." "Well what is wrong with glasses, Kitty asks. "Glasses give me a headache. Kitty, after lunch asks, where will we ski this afternoon with your folks?" Sally suggests, "How about off lift number 10 or 24?" For three days these bombers cruised the slopes. They gave skiers room when they passed by. Even Greta and Jude remarked, "Those three certainly are having a good time. Well they have a real skiing friend for the next years.

Jude replies, "I have the feeling our daughter is trying to set her brother up with girls. She has girls around the house and he never dates any of those girls Sally picks out and they all but hang on him.

"Jude, I think it runs in your blood line. I finally gave upon you for over a year before we dated. I feel sorry for any girl dating Cooper today."

"I always thought that my approach, Greta, was a good well thought out idea."

Summer came quick. Terri McGill, on a Saturday morning in early June, picked up Greta, Sally and Cooper. They drove to La Mesa and to a Western Clothing store. Terri was greeted by the owners as old friends.

Terri tells the owners, "Fix up my friends with good working clothes. Nothing fancy. There is no dancing at night or on the weekend. I want these three to be my hard working cowhands."

From boots, pants, shirts, jackets and tent like rain coats and Western hats, they tried them all on. Greta remarks, "Terri, our rain coats are certainly large."

Terri explains, "The old story about wearing cowboy rain coats is,"

'I sure can't feel who's the horse or who's the cowboy when you got those rain coats on.'"

"Cowboy raincoats have to cover your saddle and legs and boots if it's a real rain storm. You sure don't want your boots full of water that day and the days to come. Boots are tough to dry out."

"While on the ranch, when it's not raining, but working with your horse, just roll that rain cape up and tie it behind your saddle. Otherwise, you'll have soaking 'Drizzling Charlie's' and it can be a long way from the barn."

"All sporting goods stores will have a number of water kits. Get two water purification kits."

Cooper speaks up, Dr. McGill, I have two, one for Sally and me. I'll pick one out for Mom."

"Dr. McGill shakes her head. "I should have known, Cooper, as long as I have known you, you are always prepared every time. Good for you Coop."

Sally nods in agreement, then adds, Dr. McGill, you should have seen some of his girl friends. Finally I had pick out his girl friends for him.

"Sally", came the voice of Cooper. "Remember, who lets you sit on the team bench when I'm playing and you even get to me?"

It was one long afternoon trying on clothes and it finally ends. Greta suggests, "Let's pick up some Chinese food. I don't feel like cooking tonight. Terri, next week we leave. Is there anything else we need?"

"Hmm. Thought Dr. McGill. Coop. Do you have three or four water canisters?"

"I have four in my room. That should handle us. Are your streams safe to fill up our water, Doctor?"

"Oh heavens, Coop, I forgot. Bring the tablets. Take enough for your mother and sister as well. We certainly can't have the 'collywobbles' on horseback."

# CHAPTER 4

TUESDAY MORNING THE THREE new cowboys and cowgirls are loading up Greta's car. She lets out with a loud voice, "Wait one minute you two.

"We need leg room to keep the back seat clear. We are not taking all those packages in the trunk with us, period."

Sally speaks up. "The car trunk is filled up, that's why we need more room, Mom."

"OK you two, come out to the car with empty hands."

Sally and Cooper arrive with empty hands. Greta is standing next to the open car trunk. "Tell me, now, what's in all those bags?"

"Mostly my clothes Mom." reports Sally. "That old brown leather thing, something or other is Cooper's"

"OK, Miss Portage what's in all those other bags?" "My extra clothes."

'Young lady, take those 'just some third and fourth extra clothes' back to your room. Only one exchange is allowed. Any thing else, we leave at home. Same for you Cooper."

Cooper mentions, "Mom, I tried to tell Sally she packed way too many clothes but she wouldn't listen."

Greta asks, "What's in that old brown paper bag, Coop?"

"Extra underwear and socks, Mom." "Would third or fourth extras be safe in saying too much?"

"Yeah, close if we wash clothes every night." "We will. take the leather bag back to your room. One extra pair of underwear and maybe three pair of socks is enough. You can wash one pair out every night along with your sister and your mother's wash."

"Kids, Just be sure you keep a clean pair of complete clothes including underwear and socks. Oh. don't forget your swim suits, sandals and a big towel.

"With Miss Sally Portage shedding a lot of extra and unneeded clothes stuffed in the back seat, we'll have a more comfortable back seat for naps. Sally, are you ready?"

Greta informs her two charges, "I'll drive until we reach Interstate Highway 5 and 99. That's just after we leave the Grapevine. We'll be in the Greater San Joaquin Valley" Before leaving San Diego, check your maps to see where we are going. We have reservations at a motel just past the city of Sacramento. Good time to know how the middle of our state looks like.

"We'll spend the night in a motel and leave early in the morning. Should be at the ranch before or just after lunch.

Coop you have your license, I hope? You will drive from where Highway 5 and Highway 99 meet. I'll take over as we near Sacramento. Any questions. "OK gang we are off."

Four hours into the ride came a gas stop and a change in the driver. The highway appears to be flat.

Sally mentions, "Gee Coop you're sure driving differently from those three weekends at Mr. Bob Morelli's ranch."

"Morelli's Ranch?" Greta half turns to look at her daughter. She asks. "What do you mean driving at Morelli's Ranch. I know him. He was once a contractor of sorts. He did all kinds of jobs. His grandson is David Morelli; didn't you two spend some time during the summer on his grandfather's ranch."

Cooper replies, "We sure did, Mom." Sally interjects, "Yeah, Coop, and David drove two dump trucks as we helped Dad Morelli put in a new road to his ranch. He lets us drive his equipment right, Coop?"

Greta interrupts, "Wait. Are you telling me, Sally, you drove a truck on his ranch?"

"No Mom, no truck. Coop and David drove those dump trucks filling in the low spots that I missed."

"What do you mean, the low spots you missed, Sally?" Cooper says, "Sally, better tell Mom what you drove on those weekends."

"A nearly thirteen year-old girl driving what, Sally?" Greta is shocked and wants an answer. "What did you drive, Sally?"

"Well, all right. I drove a yellow D something 10 or 12 Diesel Caterpillar tractor. Big guy and I had to climb up on the tracks to drive the big tractor with a big blade in front and something in back like a big roller and a scrapper.

"Mom, I could lift up a huge big front blade when I wanted to back up or angle it when going ahead, if I were told what to do. Man-O-man, it was a real big blade in the front. I could raise it up or let it down. I could push the dirt anywhere Mr.Morelli pointed to where he wanted it placed. It was sure lots of fun, Mom."

Cooper adds, Mr. Morelli told me he just wished he had Sally working for him when he was in the contracting business. He said, "Sally was the quickest person he ever had that picked up driving that big tractor." He also said, "Your sister is a born-natural tractor driver."

Mr. Morelli couldn't drive his tractor because of his back.

Greta leans back in the back car seat. "I just can't believe my daughter, a 13 year old, was once a tractor driver and her brother let her do it."

Sally exclaims, "Mom, all the controls were so easy to use. Just about the flick of a finger was needed.

Greta doesn't really know how to punish Cooper for allowing his thirteen year-old sister to do some crazy thing like that. She briskly asks, "Cooper, didn't you become concerned about your sister getting hurt."

"A little bit at the start. But Mr. Morelli kept saying to me, 'Your sister is a natural.'"

"Also, I thought, with her eyes, this opportunity will not come again." Greta snaps "OK. We'll drop the subject now and forever. Are there any questions about that matter?"

Greta gives driving orders, "Cooper you are driving. Stay at 55 miles per hour. This is a four lane road and I don't care how fast the trucks are going, you'll drive at 55 period. I just can't believe what I just heard. Our Sally, is the tractor driver."

After a night in Sacramento, the three progress up Highway 5 the next day with Greta driving. She is still shocked when she thinks about her daughter driving a huge tractor.

After leaving Sacramento still on Highway 5, they are heading toward Fort Jones and then were promised, "You see Mt. Shasta in the distance." They are now driving between Trinity and the Sierra Mountains.

Shasta Mountain sits alone in the upper Sacramento Valley.

Sally asks, "Mom, do people really ski on that mountain you called Mount Shasta?" "Certainly." "Maybe we should have brought our skis along and had Dad with us." Greta answers that question. "With skis clothes and then all our western clothes, I don't think we would have any room in this car to enjoy the views.

Sally asks, "Is this the tallest mountain in California?" "Not by some 300 feet. Mt. Whitney on the back side of the Sierra is the tallest mountain in the Continental United States." "How do know that?" Mom, questions Sally.

"Before you two were born, Cooper, your father and I hiked up Mt. Whitney."

"You and Dad climbed up our tallest mountain?" "Sorry, no, there is a trail you follow. All types of people walk up Mt.

Whitney. It is just a long walk and there are many steps in places. I've been told all kinds of people walk up Whitney, even nudists, people with canes, with crutches, and even some bare footed hikers show up.

"There's even a ranger station, this station is the highest ranger station in our country, at 10,000 ft. elevation. When we did it, we met the ranger and his wife. She told me. "I hang up the highest American laundry in the world."

Sally replies. "Gee maybe Dad, you, Coop and I, can take that trail some time-like soon, all of us."

Sally continues, "Just to walk among the trees and see those forest views. Oh, just be up here in the spring with all those wild flowers and even smell the forest What a sight."

Cooper looks at his mother. With his right hand he fishes around the front seat for something.

Greta opens her purse an hands Cooper some tissues and takes a couple for herself.

In a crackled voice, Cooper asks, "How far before we reach Fort Jones?

Greta wipes her nose and mentions "Up ahead is Yreka, Cooper, you'll take over the driving from Yreka to Fort Jones to Etna, and then there will be a dirt road to the ranch."

Sally asks, "I know we are in California and I'm trying to find on this map where Dr. McGill's ranch is."

"OK, find Yreka first on the map. That's still on Highway 5. Then catch highway 3 going 'kinda' south to Fort Jones, got it? We'll have lunch in Fort Jones if we have time."

"Yeah, aren't we going back south, Mom." "Just a tad. Do you see Scott Bar Mountains and Marble Mountains Wilderness and the town named Etna?"

"Let's see, I got it. Etna is there." "OK Coop. We'll drive through Etna and one mile on your right will be a dirt road. Look for a sign on a post or tree with a sign spelling out McGill."

With lunch over, the three travelers found the dirt road with the McGill sign nailed onto a pine tree. "Cooper," Greta tells her son, "Drive slowly. This is a ranch road so don't scrape the bottom of my car and watch that you aren't dragging a ton of dust behind you."

Sally speaks up, "Oh, boy. Maybe if they have my kind of tractor, I can level their bouncy road."

Greta, in the front seat, quickly turns around and looks at her daughter, "Not even over my dead body!"

After a long half hour of slow driving, they arrive in at huge parking area with an old remodeled two-story house with a porch on three sides and the second story has a glassed in porch going around three sides. Greta remarks, "The second story of the house is our sleeping quarters. We'll haul all our stuff out of the car.

Terri is running from the house to greet Greta. She points toward a large 4-door blue pickup with a long blue painted horse trailer hooked on to it.

She says "Glad your here. Park your car next to the blue pickup with that long horse trailer.

"Coop will sleep in the trailer with Butch. There are four bunk beds, a toilet and a shower that the boys will use. "Roberto and his wife Tommy are coming in later with their two boys, Thomas and James. We all thought having the boys together would be better.

"We girls have the upstairs porch to ourselves. We will have showers. The boys will have a shower in the horse trailer or the creek. They are tough, they can take the cold stream water.

"Oh, Roberto and Tommy have a small cabin on the other side of our house."

Greta asks, "How old are all the children?" Terri frowns thinking. Lets see, Sally you are now 13, Virginia "Maggy" Merryweather is 14, and Maxwell "Butch" Merryweather is 17, and Tommy is 14 and his brother James is 15 years old. Those two boys will be up later. So, we have soon a group of six young adults all about the same age." Terri continues, "My brother will divide the boys up when we start gathering the cattle. I never told you, but Franco was one good football player at Duke. His playing weight in college was 278 pounds and he had sprinter speed and played as a fullback.

"Today he has about ten extra pounds on now. Right now Franco is in town getting supplies with Lee Wong, our cook.

"They should be back within the hour. I know Lee has dinner almost ready if Franco has anything to say about that, and he usually does."

A large, heavy built young man approaches Cooper. They shake hands. He tells Cooper. "I'm Butch."

"Put it there, Cooper. Terri has sent me almost everyone of your sports clippings. Holy smokes, Coop, you're some football player and a soccer star, as well."

Cooper smiles. "Not quite. That's a lot of paper talk, Butch." "My aching butt. Terri has kept me up on her observations watching you in football and soccer. Colleges should be hanging around your house."

"Not quite, but I've heard the same about you. You got a college picked out now?"

"Yeah, I think. UC at Berkeley looks good. They don't have a pile of linemen on hand like USC.

"Correct. I'm going to Cal Poly in San Luis Obispo next fall. They have a super engineering architect program I like. Also there's good surf at Avila Beach, a few miles away from the campus. I just have to keep my board in shape."

"Butch, I'm not interested in making football or soccer a life time occupation. My sister at her age is already receiving lots of interest from the Trojans and other colleges and universities, regarding her swimming.

"But isn't she having a problem with her eyes?" "Yeah, but it's the swimming records she is grabbing up already." Butch replies, "That's right, Coop. Terri is so proud of Sally, that she feels she will make the Olympic team in her first year in college. That is four years from now, Butch.

"Sally is one tough competitor. That's the strange thing about her. She refuses to talk to any competitor before the race. After the race she considers every competitor a friend, but not before."

"Coop, I never could do that in my two sports. How do you rate Sally's eyes?"

"Her vision is disappearing slowly to the family. But, if you haven't seen her for a while, then it seems fast. She has blind spots and more gray is showing up in her vision.

"We are doing everything to keep her on track and staying with projects from keeping her room exactly with everything in its place, to climbing ladders, reading braille, to cooking, and to washing dishes as well as mountain climbing."

"Wait a minute, Cooper. Your sister, Sally, is climbing mountains and has a seeing problem?

"Yep, she loves it. Either I or another climber, one will take the lead and other takes the belay. We haven't dropped her yet, nor will we." "Butch, she's one tough lady. Also she's darn good in self protection. That was my idea. She already has a black belt. If any one she doesn't know makes a move on Sally's body, then he will usually land on his back. She's quick."

"Wow, Cooper, So when her vision goes, she will be ready and not end up being a crippled person."

"Exactly. She knows certain things she can't do, but other things she can handle. Fortunately her classmates, boys included, watch her constantly to prevent a problem from occurring from walking to meeting strangers. Everyone in school watches out for Sally.

"She even dates and dances. Her classmates, keep her up on the new dances. Sally even shows me many of the new dances."

Butch suggests, "Do you think I can get a couple of dances with Sally while we are on this ranch?"

"I'm sure she would be proud to teach you a couple of new steps. That is, if I let her."

"Coop. Your my type of guy." A girl hollers, "You guys want dinner or are you two eating with the horses?" Butch tells Cooper "That's my sister." Another call came, "Coop, I'm very hungry. Can I have your dinner as well?"

"Butch, that's my sister." Five o'clock in the morning came early to the new riders. Butch shook Cooper awake. "Time to do our chores, cowboy."

"We have eight horses to feed, then groom. Do you think our sisters will be around this early? Nope, they will sleep in this morning."

Cooper and Butch walk over to the barn to feed their horses. Cooper hollers, "Butch, you told me last night you put the horses in those stalls at the end of the barn?

"That's right. The eight on the north end." "No way, chief. The way I see it there's no horses I can see." Butch stares down the empty stalls where Cooper is standing and the stall doors are open. "Coop, I'll look out into the corrals. I know I put them in those stalls before I fed them. Maybe they wandered out, some how." About four minutes later Butch yells out. "Our two backward sisters have all of our horses over here being fed now. Guess who gets to curry them?"

"Butch, any chance they will do that every morning?" "No, but we'll hear that story for days. Your sister just told me to have breakfast and eat fast. They want us to curry and saddle all the horses. Shall I throw these two girls in the pond now or later?"

"Sally should know, Butch, It's a long road that doesn't have a turn in it." After a breakfast of eggs and hot cakes, the four stuff their saddle bags with sandwiches and ride out to see the ranch on horse back.

Butch and Maggy watched Cooper and Sally saddle up under the careful eye of Terri and Greta. Thankfully the riding lesson at Otay Lakes, which Terri suggested, worked.

Maggy and Butch will show the two Portages parts of the ranch.

The four are on a scouting trip this day. While keeping their horses going higher up the ranges, then the views and areas of interest are pointed out to Sally and Cooper.

Cooper asks, Butch, "Who owns all this land?

Butch replies, "This is government land. The McGills pay the government so much a head to have this land. The government requires only so many head, of cattle or horses, per 100 acres.

"Coop, there is a group of cattle owners using all this land. When roundup time comes, starting two days from now, all the cattle will be gathered up and separated by brands, the calves branded, and all are given shots in a dusty manure ground. And that is exactly what we'll be doing."

"Then Coop, it's from daylight to dark for us. Your rear end will know it from day one to the finish."

"Yep. but the cattle don't know the rules. We may find cattle 50 miles away from their range. Yep, even some of ours will be over somewhere else. Cattle ranchers are honest and at the end of every area we clean out, then the ownership is straightened out.

"Last year, Maggy and I spent two days herding about 50 head of our cattle back to the McGill's range."

"Butch, what did you do at night?" "Slept out. We carried prepared food. It's a long haul. If we do it this year, I'll ask for you and Sally to go with us. It's a great ride and there are a couple of lakes to cool off in."

"Then no one else can be on this land so to speak, Butch?" "Parts of the area are open for hunters of deer or bear, or fishermen.

But they have to clear with the rangers. Where we are now is not for hunting or fishing. There are all kinds of signs saying no fishing or hunting allowed. That's if people can read signs."

"Why, Butch?" "Because there are too many trees and there's a lack of water. Franco has tapped some water and made some areas to bring water to the cattle. So hunting and fishing is not allowed. Just our selected cattle are allowed.

"No cars, trucks or any other vehicles are allowed in this surrounding area.

"That's why Maggy and I made the long trip by horseback. To truck those cattle would have been horrendous in miles. It was a short cut for us."

"The four teen age riders covered as much land as they would be riding in two days. All four mentioned to each other "My butt is sore. We only have a couple of days to get in shape." So they walked their horses whenever they could.

While walking their horses down one of the last arroyo's closest to the ranch house, Maggy calls out, "Butch, Cooper, come over here."

Butch and Cooper ride over to where Sally and Maggy wait. She points to the ground. "Look, these tire tracks are fresh."

Butch hands his reins to Cooper, after he jumps off his horse. Butch looks very carefully then tells the group, "Your right Sis, they are tire tracks but I don't think they are tracks from a pickup or a car. Look at that Coop, they are certainly vehicle tracks. We'll alert Franco about these tracks. They certainly are not old tracks either."

Butch starts to follow the tracks. Cooper suggests "Could those tracks be from a short coupled vehicle, one of those cut down and made over vehicles, Butch?"

"I think you got it, Coop. Some one has been sneaking in here and hunting right under Franco nose. Wait till we tell him, he's going to explode."

Cooper suggests, "You know Butch these tracks look new and some appear to be older. Someone has been here a couple of times. That salt lick there should bring cows and deer to this area. A silent gadget on the muzzle of a rifle would prevent anyone at the ranch from hearing a shot. Those tuys are kinda skillful creatures."

"Mighty good thinking Coop. Lets saddle up and we'll let Franco know what we saw and think."

Four riders returned to the ranch sooner than expected. Franco is in his office with Terri and Greta looking at some old photos.

Butch reports what the four riders found and what Cooper supposed happened. Franco paces the floor. He thinks out loud. "With a good exhaust system we wouldn't hear the vehicle. And with a silencer on a rifle, who would hear a vehicle. So we have someone on our ranch that is not supposed to be here with a rifle." Terri suggests, "I'll call the sheriff tomorrow morning Franco. Maybe Sheriff Tate might like to know this has been happening to other ranchers as well."

"OK, Sis. We got kids here. When you guys are out riding tomorrow stay away from that area, understand?"

All four nod in agreement.

In the late afternoon, the horses were unsaddled, washed down, and hooked up to a walking wheel to dry off and cool down. Then the riders fed all their horses. After showers and dinner, the two boys and their sisters didn't stay up late this night.

In the morning four riders took new horses and prepared to take another ride. Franco dug out two, two-way radios. He tells them, "Any problems, contact me.

He hands one to Butch and the other to Maggy. "If there are any suspicious acts call me. Just don't be a hero. Call me and don't go to that area today. Do you understand?"

All four agreed. "Which way are you four going this morning?" Butch says, "Over toward section 23 to 56. We should be back around four." "OK. Remember, if there's anything you think is not right or smells bad, leave the area and call me."

# CHAPTER 5

As the four riders move out, Butch suggests, "Mag, take Sally and ride over toward Jensen's Falls. That should be about a four hour ride. We'll meet at the Falls."

"OK, Boss man. If anything different shows up, I'll give you a call." "One more thing. If there is any slight suspicious sign, get on the radio and call us. Can you follow those orders, sister?" "What kind of creature you think I am. No problem, brother. It's not your football you're talking to. It's two smart girls.

'I know that's tough to understand, but we do have brains." "I had no doubts. Maybe give us a call, say, every half hour and Coop and I will call you two on the fifteen minutes of the hour. Can you follow that?"

"It's much better than when your team forgot the signals and the play you wanted cost us the Championship."

"You still are digging me about that? Remember, keep in radio contact with us. See you two in four hours."

As the two teams rode off going in opposite directions, Cooper leans over his saddle and said, "One play and you lost the game?"

"Yeah. Five seconds to go. They had a lucky field goal earlier. We are on their one foot line. Coop, that's the one foot line. "I'm the captain and normally play defense. Our offense tackle is out so I'm going both ways. I called our last time out. I gathered the team together and went over this trick play we didn't use the whole game.

Every one understood it, I thought. And I even made our Quarterback repeat it twice to me.

"Coop it's a walk through play. Easy. We split our offense line giving our linemen good angles on blocks. Our center line averages 215 pounds per man.

"Our quarterback gets the ball, from the center, and says later, 'I just forget to follow our left guard,'

"Well this guard is fast off the blocks, and weighs 198 pounds. "Our quarterback, who always wants to be the big show, is to follow the pulling guard into the number two hole on the right side. "Instead of going right, Our showboat tries left. I guess he wants all the glory. So he meets our pulling guard head on, behind the line of scrimmage.

"The game is over. We lost 3 zip." That's what my sister alluded to:

'Get the directions correct and follow them." Coop and Butch ride along trading football notes and plays. Two hours pass. Only three calls, by radio, come from the girls.

Cooper asks Butch, aren't we supposed to have a call from the girls by now?"

"Darn right, Coop. They are ten minutes late. I called twice. The last call sounded like someone turned off the radio. It sounded liked a click. Lets go find them."

Cooper rides up close to Butch. "I would suggest no more calls. Lets eye ball first."

"Good idea Coop. You are a thinker I could have used you on our last play. What a dumb quarterback." Then Butch spits on the ground.

They pass through a number of small valleys. If looking at the worst they may have met up with the people that should not be on the ranch. "I saw your 10 power binoculars yesterday. You got them with you, Coop?" "Yep, want it?" "No Keep it handy. Let me go over this. Where would those two girls be, say one hour ago. Probably on section 15. Another fifteen minutes they would still be in that valley. I'm thinking the worst Coop. Lets go around and come up from the back about the same route our girls might have taken."

"Butch, that idea is better than a wild guess. Lets go."

The two boys bring their horses in a round half circle. Cooper leaves his horse. He tells Butch, "I'm going to check and see if we are right. Cooper climbs through a wooded side going to the top of the ridge. Then, taking out his 10-power binoculars, he focuses in on two men appearing to be talking to their sisters.

Cooper searches beyond and finally sees the two horses, with saddles on tied to a tree using their reins, not the short rope around the necks of the horses belonging to the girls.

Cooper, with limited horse riding experience, knows that is wrong.

He slides back down the wooded bank and meets with Butch. "The girls are there with two men. Their horses are tied to a tree about fifty yards from the girls. Who ever tied up the horses used the reins and not the cotton rope."

Butch replies, "Coop, I know Mag would never tie her horse to anything using her reins. Those are leather hand braided reins, her best and she is as finicky as a mother bear with her cub about those reins. Something is dead wrong.

"Coop. Did you see any guns?" "I sure did. Both men have rifles. It appears they have our sisters hostage." "Give me the glasses. I want to see it myself." "Just be careful, Butch. Don't let the girls see you." "Right. It won't take long. Think of something we can to do to free the girls." Butch disappears into the dark steep forested area. About ten minutes later, Butch returns. "Damn it, they are still talking. Any ideas?" "Butch, why are they still talking?" "Coop, that doesn't figure. Unless the girls are trying to talk themselves out of a problem. How close do you think we can get to those men and surprise them?"

"Running in cowboy boots will be tough. If those guys would set their rifles down we might have a chance.

Cooper touches Butch's arm. "You know Butch, this sounds crazy. Our two girls aren't dumb. If those men turn around to see us coming at them, I'm sure those girls will do something like scratch their eyes out."

Butch asks, "What do you think, ride our horses or try to sneak up on the men getting as close as we can?"

"Hmm. Butch, I'm not the horse rider you are. Let me get as close to the men by sneaking up on them. Watch me signal with my hand.

"Then make your charge. You will come up the valley screaming your head off. I'm sure our girls will jump into the battle. You will be coming at them on their left.

"I'll be behind them when they turn to see you. Look dangerous. I'll run down the valley. I'll try for a rabbit punch on one or both of them. Better yet, you take the guy I didn't punch, take him out by punching or let your horse do the damage."

Butch hits Coops shoulder. "You're on buddy. Give me four minutes to make your signal for my charge."

"OK, Butch, but don't try to do the hero routine and go the wrong way?"

"Now it's you. Watch me." Cooper heads up the wooded hill to try to get as close he can unseen.

As he wiggles through the brush he's thinking, No snakes, no noise. That guy is watching the girls.

One man, the taller of the two, steps toward Sally as she steps back. He's only able to grab her shirt. With a pull on her shirt, it rips her shirt nearly off.

Coming around the bend is Butch, He just saw what happened. Sitting on his saddle and swinging his rope overhead, he is hollering and yelling at the top of his voice. He lets his lariat go. This catches the tall man right around his waist.

Immediately his horse breaks to the left, as any well trained team roping horse is trained to do, and is now pulling the man along.

Coop was taking off like a sprinter leaving his blocks. He charges the man that was going after Maggy. She quickly turned around, took three steps and kicks the man just missing his crotch. But her boot slammed into his stomach.

With that one kick by Maggy, he stumbles and falls to the ground. Then staggers up on his feet.

Copper sprinting the best he can in cowboy boots slams into the back of this man's legs. To Cooper the man appeared to reach for Maggy or was going to try and leave. Either way, according to Cooper, he wasn't.

Over with Butch and Sally the roped stranger, with a loop around his knees, wobbles as he stands up. Butch quickly flips a hitch over this man's body confining his arms. Then the last thrown put a hitch around the man's neck.

This man tries to take a step toward Butch's horse who immediately backs up knocking the man to the ground.

The Junior Championship Rodeo steer roper walks up to the tightly bound stranger.

He says to the tied up stranger, "Just try to untie yourself and my horse will drag your body clear back to the ranch. Just remember what I said."

While Butch was playing cowboy, Cooper had given his man a perfect clip behind his knees and the man is now rolling around the grass and moaning. Cooper is deciding where to kick him next.

Maggy pulls Cooper away. "Coop. I don't think he is going any where with a perfect illegal football clip. "I'll bet this stranger's knees were ripped from his tendons. He's sure crying out with intense pain.

Now Maggy looks around, squints, then comments, "Four of us sure cleaned up two guys good and proper."

Four young people stand for a moment or two looking at the crying poachers in pain. Then the girls hug each other and cry.

The boys grab each other around the shoulders. "Damn good job" they say to each other.

Cooper picks up the two rifles and then makes two loops, similar to Butches loops. Then he sticks his man's feet and boots through through the two hitches and tightens up the hitches by having his horse back up. He is just following Butches act. Butch tells the two men, "One move that I don't like from either one of you guys that I think might concern me or my friends, we'll do something Indian fashion.

"Or, will drag you both behind our horses to the ranch. Either way you'll arrive good and dead. "Don't talk, and don't move other wise our horses will give both an Indian style ride until you are in pieces."

Butch calls Franco on the radio. "Franco, we are with the girls. All is well. We have two poachers taken care of. I think an ambulance should be called and your sheriff notified. We'll wait till you arrive or should we drag the men in.

"What did you say over the air?"

"Oh besides that, can you bring Sally another one of her shirts? Nope.

What? What was that you said? We are grown up young adults. We just did the job you told us to do. How long do we have to wait?

"Coop and I are ready and can drag these guys to your ranch. No, we can't. I think that Coop took one of them guys, both knees out. He's really hurting."

News of catching two rustlers rolled out in local news papers, radios and one TV station.

Maggie came up to Sally and whispered "Do you want some nice western clothes?"

"Sure Maggie, but how?" "Have your mother sign this contract allowing you to have some TV pictures taken in town. He will pay us in western clothes. One or both of the women TV camera operators will be with us during the shoots. Just have your mom sign it. Mine did."

At six in the morning a station wagon rolls into the wide parking area of the McGill Ranch.

Two girls leave the station wagon saying "Thank you." Then they came into the huge dining room.

Greta, Terri, and some other cowboys are having breakfast. Two tired girls dropped their large clothing bags on the floor. Each said "Good Night" and mentioned, "Please let us sleep through breakfast and lunch. We had a long night. See you." And off the girls go slowly climbing the stairs to their second cots.

Terry jumps up and starts to look at the western clothes the girls brought back from the TV station shots.

"Holy Cow, would you look what our cowgirls walked away with. These items will never see sales. I guess our girls know good fashion."

Cooper and Sally are coming up to the end of their cowboy punching, stay. This particular evening all the riders were being congratulated by Terri and Franco. The round up was perfect.

The telephone rang in Franco's study. He returns to the living room. "With a commanding voice, Franco orders "Sally, Maggy, Butch and Coop, don't unsaddle your horses. I have a job for you four. "The rest of us will follow behind. Sheriff Tate was on the phone. A five year old girl named Annica is lost. She was last seen playing around that long narrow valley we call Long Valley.

"I want you four to go and split the narrow valley. You can take flashlights. Don't use your flashlights before she is found.

Go two on one side and two on the other side. Walk your horses slowly. Watch your horses ears. Butch take

Cooper and Maggie take Sally. You two have done it before.

Here's the radios. We will get organized and follow. Tito has some sandwiches to give you. Any questions?"

Sally speaks up. Can I take one of your Collie pups with me. I've heard puppies work well with children lost in forest areas."

Franco looks at Sally and then his sister. "Terry have you heard anything about that for a lost child?"

"No, but try it. Get that God awful friendly light colored pup and give it to Sally. Oh, and a leash too."

Maggie, Butch, Cooper and Sally along with the pup leave the house. As they walk to their horses, Cooper asks, "Sally, hand me the pup. It will be easier for you to climb on your horse."

Cooper holds the wiggling pup until Sally mounts. Cooper comments, "I guess he wants you."

"OK gang let's go." orders Butch, "Lets move out." There's no moon tonight—just stars as they walk their horses. It's a quiet night. There's no talking amongst the four riders. The pup that Sally has is quite content to remain in Sally's arms.

After about fifteen minutes the four riders reach the spot suggested by Franco. The four bring their horses close together.

Butch, with a whisper announces, "Maggie and Sally this is your side to cover. Walk your horses slowly. If the girl is here we don't want to scare her. Do not talk tough. These are the rules. "Sally, you have the pup. Watch the pup as well. Don't ride too close to the ravine. We don't want to scare the little girl. Maggie, stay about five or ten feet from Sally.

"Coop and I will be on the other side. Give a whistle, not a long one or loud, if you think you found her. Lets go. We'll whistle when we are ready on our side. OK, ladies, good hunting.

Cooper and Butch ride around the beginning of the arroyo splitting the two pastures. Butch whistles and Maggie whistles the return. The hunt begins.

Maggie whispers to Sally, "Don't get too close to the edge you may scare the girl, Annica. Watch your horses ears and the pups ears.

"When you think you see or notice something whistle to me. Butch just whistled, the hunt is on."

There is no talking. Slowly, the four tired riders, trying to stay alert, walk their horses and watch their ears.

Twenty minutes have passed and there is no sign of anyone in the wide ravine. Sally's horse and Maggie's horse's ears wiggle. Both girls stop their horses and wait. Maggie moves up close to Sally and whispers, "You got a bite?"

Sally returns with her whisper, "I think so. My horse just snorted and the pup is squirming, Mag."

"Hand me the pup and your reins and dismount. Then I'll give you the pup. Don't go yet. I'm going with you."

"What about the horses, Mag?" Maggie quietly answers. "My horses are trained not to move when the reins are dropped. When goat tying I don't want my horse to run away. Let's go, you have the pup."

The two girls walk with the pup on a leash slowly and begin to walk to the edge of the sloping ravine.

Maggie nudges Sally indicating to start talking. "Annica, my sister and I have a puppy for you." There's some movement in the brush. Maggie, with a whisper, says, Here's your new puppy, Annica. Catch him honey. Let the pup go, Sally." Sally is on the ground and reaches for the pup. Maggie cautions Sally, "Go slow and easy sister as we don't want her to run and hide. Watch your pup. Go slowly."

Sally, holding the leash walks toward the ravine watching the pups ears and his body movement. She quietly says, "Annica, your mommy has a puppy for you. Dinner is ready. My sister and I will take you to your mommy with your new puppy."

There is not a sound. In two more steps Sally is about five feet from the bushes. "I'm getting hungry, Annica, and you are."

Sally thought she saw some movement of some brush. Sally let loose of the pup's leash. The dog makes a dash into the brush.

"Here he is, honey." So carefully walking out of the thick grass and brush a child pushes the vegetation slowly apart and reaches the edge of the pasture.

The puppy did its job by jumping up on Annica's face with kisses. Sally bends over and picks up Annica while the puppy is still kissing her, and Sally walks carefully over to Maggie.

Sally asks, "Look what we have. Our evening was better than stealing our brother's clothes, Maggie."

"I'll hold Annica. Get on your horse and I'll hand you Annica and a pup." Maggie hollers over to Butch. "Big brother, grab the horn and tell Franco we have Annica and her new pup. We five plus Liana's pup are coming home."

The farm house is lit up with lights and cars and pickups. When the four riders enter the parking circle: Cheers come along with the parents of Annica, crying.

Three news paper reporters and one photographer, two radio station people, and that good looking young TV man and his staff are all smiling and cheering, flashing cameras lights and the TV people all smiling with the blinking lights brightening up the steps and people waving their hands.

Sally whispers in Maggie's ear. "Do we have time to change into our new clothes?"

Franco was called out by the reporters to interview him as to just how the search was started how the child was found so fast with his staff.

Franco looks around and there are no girls. He walks over to his sister, Terri, where's our girls?"

"Big brother you have never learned this rule about women: "Never be caught on film unless you are dressed correctly." Our girls will be down soon.

Our boys were also in the search. You might lay on the reporters the boys athletic abilities while we wait for the girls."

Terri puts her fingers in her mouth and lets out a shrill whistle: When the jostling reporters quiet down.

She announces: "You reporters might be interested, but this is what good athletics can do and they can think fast.

This big guy standing next to me, Franco McGill, his last name is one word, was once an All American Football player at Duke Univ. and is a Silver Star recipient in Korea.

"Now you have the old athletic and the new athletic guys in front of you. Meredith Merryweather, or Butch to us, is an All California High School Defensive Tackle and a Wrestler and is entering USC this fall. Also, he's one half of the Junior National Team Roping Championship.

"Standing on Meredith's right side is Geraldo Cooper Portage. He will enter Cal Poly in San Luis Obispo, as a Freshman.

"He will carry to Cal Poly: All California Soccer player and the owner of the highest points in all California High School Varsity in Soccer as well as football. Both of these lads are in the top ten percent of their graduating class.

"Coming down the stairs, On your right is Virginia, or better known as Maggie Merryweather, a sophomore in high school, the one with the dark hair, is an All Star High School goat tier, and barrel racer.

Next to her, the natural blond, is Sally Wilhelmina Portage, an eighth grade swimmer as our Champion Sprint Racer. Notice that the two girls changed into their new Western outfits just for you."

Terri continues, "We are going to celebrate tonight that Annica was located after wandering away, and when found was given the Shepherd pup she's now holding.

"Come on in we have plenty of food for everyone." The celebration lasted until daylight. Franco McGill was cornered by the newspaper and television people then Sheriff Tate, along with the Superintendent of the National Forest. They pleaded with Franco and Terri McGill to consider developing their ranch into a year around resort, like a Dude Ranch.

Franco replies, "Only if Lee Wong, Tito and Jessie become our partners. Neither Terri nor I can even boil water without burning it."

Sheriff Tate asks "Oh, Terri, where's our girls?" "Tate, you just don't know girls. You only had boys. The TV people have taken the girls into town for more pictures and interviews at their TV Station. "Again, that young good looking TV director mentioned something about opening that large western store for the girls. "Those two girls knew exactly how to get what they wanted. New clothes. Those two gals are sharp. They informed the TV director, "If you want to talk to me? I have to see, again, some clothes. Good for those gals."

All the way home, to San Diego, Sally is talking about her western clothes. "Just wait till Dad sees them."

Greta grits her teeth. She knew some time she has to tell and this must be the time. "Well, kids, your father may not be home when we arrive."

Cooper asks, "Oh, is he on another trip, Mom?" "Uh, I don't know." Sally, sitting in the back seat, leans forward, with her arms looped over the back of the front seat. "Are you telling us Dad has moved out, Mom?"

"Uh, well, something like that. He's traveling a lot now and will continue this traveling for some time. We talked about it and decided it may best best for us to separate for a while."

Sally's voice is cracking. "Mom, you mean you and Dad are getting a divorce?" She sniffles.

"Wait a minute. We haven't gone that far yet, Lady." Cooper wades in, "It sure sounds like it. And nobody asked us for our opinions. That's not fair to Sally and me. Do you have another man in mind, Mom?"

"That never came up, kids, and we all know there is no one else in the picture?"

"Mom, if that is true then why the separation? If Dad were in the army fighting in some distant country, isn't that separation?"

Sally jumps in, "I don't know that, Mom. You sure were nice when Franco was around." "Franco is only a new friend, period." Sally shakes her head. "I like him but not as a father." "I told you Sally, he was nice to me, period. There's nothing else and that is the end of the subject." Greta asks, "Coop, we are about one and half hours before we're home. Do you want to drive?"

"No, thank you." It was a long hour and a half with no talking. Greta asks, "You guys want to listen to some music you brought with you?" There was not a sound from the two. Both are spending this quiet time looking out their side of the car windows. All conversation has stopped.

Four years have passed, Christmas is days away. Sally is now a senior in high school. She and her mother are sitting in their living room and appear to be waiting for something. Not a light in the house is on. Even the Christmas tree lights are off.

"Mom, can I turn the lights on now?" "Hmmm, I guess so. Punch the lights on, dear." Sally takes her cane and walks over to the front door. She flips the switch.

Greta looks at her Christmas tree effort. "Well, not bad. But your father always did a better job with the lights."

"Will you two ever get together again, Mom?" "That is something we still have to work out ourselves, nosey." "Well, it's family and that is important. Every Christmas I always made a wish you two would patch things up and get back together. Each Christmas I had my fingers crossed and then, blah." "For a young lady that can't see, you sure know what's going on in other peoples lives. Let me now say something and it's just between us, who just happens to be your Mother. "Remember Miss Portage, after your Winter Formal dance you were, that's you young lady, a good one hour past your curfew time to be home.

"Remember, I never said a word and you haven't had another date with Chester. Now, can you tell your Mother what you two were doing to stay out way past your promised time to be home? That's this home, remember your last words to me?"

"I'll be home after the dance." Sally replies. "Well, Chester's folks called me thinking you two were here. I felt stupid as I didn't know and one person, I know, didn't think to use her telephone because it was never on.

"Now what were you two doing those two early morning hours?" "We were parked and talking, that's all, Mom." "Parking. Of course. Fortunately Robert's Cleaners were able to get your lipstick off from around the neckline of that beautiful light green formal of yours."

"Well, Mom, all we were doing was some kissing. Nothing below the shoulders, that's true. He had the same instructions from his folks as you gave me what time to be home. But we did a lot of talking."

"Over one hour of just talking?" "I guess so. Sure weren't like those two love birds in the back seat.

Ginger had to get out of Chester's folks car to get her formal straighten out before we took those two home. I thought it was disgusting.

"No, don't worry. They didn't go all the way. Another hour well, maybe. That's the truth why we were late."

"Hmmm. One hour to straighten her formal? That doesn't add up in my book."

"Well maybe it wasn't taking that long. Sorry we were late. I was trying to explain to Chester why we shouldn't go steady. Things were heating up too fast and too much and he wasn't buying it." "Sally, It would have been easier on me if you had told me sooner. Now turnoff the Christmas lights and we'll turn them back on when your brother arrives.

"By the way, did you give Chester a Christmas present?" "No. Well, I've been thinking something like a book on dating manners. Maybe a Christmas card with a big 'Adios" printed on it." "Normally, young lady, one breaks up a relationship after Christmas, not before." "Nope, not for me. I'm looking, well not looking I guess in that fashion, for someone that's mature and I don't know any boy in our senior class that is close to maturity that would date any girl that is blind."

"Honey, the day will come maybe a long time away, or maybe very close, that a boy will show up."

"Mother, all I want is a man like Cooper. Firm, athletic, honest, a good talker, and accept me as I am. I don't know how I look compared to other girls, well some tell me but I'm not sure if they are honest or lying.

"Well some of my real friends tell me I have a great figure and I'm good looking even with my dark glasses off. Oh, I can't tell if they are honest or being nice to me."

"They are very honest. The time will come my dear and sooner than you expect and . . .

"Shhh, Mom, I think I heard a car in the driveway. Maybe it's Cooper. "I don't want some one who thinks one date gets some kissing. The second date serious kissing. The third date French kissing and some feels.

"Then, the big fourth date or the fifth date someone better have protection. To some, they might think they can go all the the way with protection or if not then depend on luck, I mean lots of luck."

"Mom, I don't like those ideas. I'll wait till I have two rings on one finger." "Sally. Two rings on one finger. Did I hear two rings on one finger, Sally! Did I hear that correctly, Sally? "Absolutely. Oh "Mom, is that our garage door opening, that I'm hearing?" Sally and Greta wait. A minute later the garage door closes. The two ladies wait. Now there's steps on the porch. Another long wait came.

Finally the front door opens and they hear, "Merry Christmas ladies. What a beautiful tree."

Two large boxes are under Cooper's arms. "Mom, you look great and who's that blond lady that was a young girl when I left for school in August?

"What's wrong with you? Are you kissed out on your Senior Christmas Formal or did you save a kiss for your brother?"

Then came the kiss to his sister and to his Mother. Sally tells Cooper, "Your kisses certainly have improved. Do they have classes in kissing along with sex education at your college?"

"No sister, you are expected to come trained." Sally interrupts. "Coop. It's not me to discuss dear brother, it is you.

Our phone has been ringing all the time wanting you for parties. It's strange Coop, not one boy called. Do you want all those girls names before you sit down?"

"I'll wait. Let me put these two packages under the your tree. I have to go out on our porch 'cause I have to bring in something that I can't leave on the porch."

"Is it a horse, Coop?" Sally is smiling. "Just shut your eyes and wait, Sally."

"Well, all I can see is a little, well, mostly light and dark. OK, Coop, for you, I'll shut my eyes. I can't see or have you forgotten."

"Of course not, just being polite."

Cooper goes out the front door and returns carrying a large wrapped Christmas box and pushes a flashy red tandem bicycle. He shuts the front door. His mother is trying hard not to say a word.

Cooper hands his sister, rather he bumps Sally with the large Christmas wrapped box. "You can open this box tonight, if you wish or save it for Christmas? It's up to you, blonde."

Sally looks in the general direction where her mother sits. "What do you think Mom?"

Greta looks at the red hot Tandem bicycle then to the box. "Hmm. "Coop has two presents for you. Open the box. Save the other. No. Wait till morning, then open both. OK Cooper?"

"Sounds good to me." Sally adds, "You guys are sure mean to me, can't I even feel around a present or two?" Two "No's" Sally heard.

# CHAPTER 6

In the morning Cooper comes down the stairs. "Thank you Mom, for letting me sleep in. Is Sally still asleep?"

"No. She was turning the shower off just before I came down the stairs."

"Well, I thought Sally and I would bicycle to Yosemite after she graduates in June and before her summer swimming meet begins. Is that a good idea?"

"Wait, Coop, Bicycling alone all the way to Yosemite on that tandem is a big project for you. You know she is blind. This is different from the time when she could see, even, somewhat."

"I know that Mom. Remember I promised Sally, some years ago that this would be my graduation present to her. Maybe she has forgotten now that graduation is just six months away."

"You think your sister ever forgets? Yes. Coop, your sister keeps reminding me of your offer."

"Coop. This will be a big responsibility on your part. However, she still climbs with some of your good mountain climbing friends and the judo class is great for her.

"Charlie Chin, Sally's instructor, thinks she's the best. He keeps saying, "This spring she will have a black belt.

"Then, Sally's swimming times are explosive in the conference. There are no swimmers in Sally's dashes that can stay up with her.

"Well, it isn't one more thing for me to push out more grey hairs. "I think that tandem bicycle is one wonderful present. Coop, your sister still misses you, quit a lot." "Well I miss her, and the bike may give her a different view of what's outside." "I think you may be on the right track, Coop." "Mom, next year, I am finishing my major, and will begin some very long hours. My advanced Engineering architectural classes will become, at times, twenty-four hours and nearly seven days a week, and the grind begins in September."

"Are you happy with your choice, Coop?"

"So far I love it. I have an instructor that is something. He demands students to try something new.

I'm thinking of remaining and maybe pick up an engineering degree. When I mentioned my thoughts to Dr. Fredor Sokolov I would love to design large buildings instead of houses."

"He suggested, "Young man, I have a project for this spring if you don't mind long hours alone. I have offered this course before with no takers. Interested?"

"So Mom, I accepted." "Do you have any close girl friends, Coop." "Nope. Nothing to bring home to show off to the family anyway. Next fall there is no way to become involved with girls. I want to hit my Master's on a straight run, then some time along the line, get a Doctorate."

"Have you told your Dad your thoughts?" "Yep. We had dinner twice last month. I think he has a project he's working on, outside his company's work. "I was really surprised to see Dad in our school's coffee shop with two of our instructors in the Education Department. Is there any chance that Dad is going to be a Professor at Cal Poly in San Luis Obispo, Mom?" Greta slowly replies, "Sorry to say, I haven't heard from Jude since he told me in November, that he'll be out of the country starting from December to June or July next year. Although he did say, "This is my last trip forever. Then, he is trotting around in your school. Something is wrong here."

Cooper asks "And the future, Mom?" "I was never able to talk to Jude long enough to ask him. I know he will not be here in San Diego during this Christmas. I'll wait till your father returns for a serious talk."

"Divorce-wise Mom?" "We'll wait, Coop. Shall we have the package opening before or after breakfast?" Cooper looks over to the stack of presents under the tree. "Are some of those presents from Terri, Mom?" "Sure are, like a whole bunch."

When will Terri be here?" Greta checks her watch. "About an hour from now. She told me she had a patient to check in on before coming here."

Cooper glances at the stairs. Sally is slowly coming down the stairs using the stair's rail for support. Her feet have disappeared in the huge Jack rabbit slippers. "Let's have Sister Sally jump over the couch. I'll hand her my two presents, Mom."

Cooper rearranges his box and the shining red tandem bicycle in the living room. Now Sally is standing by the foot of the stairs.

Sally inquires, "I thought with all the noise you were making, you were doing some changes with the living room furniture."

"Well, Sister Sally, why don't you start out on this box." Cooper hands Sally a large box requiring Sally to hold this box with both hands.

"Thanks Coop. Now lead me over to my chair, please." Greta taps Sally on her shoulder. "First, a Good Morning and a kiss, Sally. Also, one for your brother." Sally completes her kisses still holding the slightly heavy box. Greta says, "My word, what a large box Santa left you, Sally. You need to open it. I'll get a knife." Greta returns and slices the box open.

Cooper suggests, "OK Sally. Here is your present. Dig them out and tells us what you have."

Sally fishes around the box. "It feels like two things alike. Two, now two metal things. No, there are four things. Yes. Two and two. Two small things each in two small packs, I guess. They feel like two back packs and two large ones. Let me think."

Sally thinks for a minute or two. Then she quietly asks, "Cooper are these packs supposed to go on bicycles, but that doesn't figure out. Wait a minute. Is there a tandem bicycle in the mix that I can't see?"

Cooper jumps up and goes over to his sister, and putting his hands around her he gives her a hug, "Sally babe, you're just too sharp to fool. Stand up and I'll show you your tandem bicycle."

"Coop, I think I know what color my tandem bicycle is? Is this the one we are taking to go to Yosemite, after my high school graduation?"

"That's it, babe. Can you tell us what color it is? "What do you think I have in my body some type type of a spiritual kink to determine the future? No way, Mr.

Portage. My favorite color, once when I could see, was red. OK, I'll guess it's a red tandem bicycle, right?"

"I should never try to fool you princess. It's your bicycle and you will have four panniers to put everything you want to take. That's with saving two panniers for the driver.

"Remember we'll sleep out, and have, at least, breakfast and dinner while camping out. On the back of your bicycle we'll pack our sleeping bags, our tent, and maybe our cooking and eating utensils."

"Suppose it rains. Coop?"

"We'll take rain clothes or I carry a poncho. It may push a little more wind but it's better ventilation while bicycling."

"OK Coop. I'll follow your advice except you are going to find boys for me."

"Sally, that figures out providing you don't go searching for a girl for me. I'll keep that search in my pocket. This gives you, my sister, six months to learn not to mess with my love life, if I ever had one."

During the last vacation week of the Christmas holidays Cooper and Sally bicycled everyday. They would pack their lunch and head off somewhere. Cooper would say, "Sally point the way we should go today."

His sister would ask, "What direction should I point? Lets find at least one ride with no hills."

"Not in this town, sister." "How about Coronado this time, Coop, and we'll take the ferry back across the bay to San Diego. "I know it's a short trip, Coop, but lets go. We can eat our lunch; wasn't there a strip of lawn splitting the main drag?"

"You're right, but just leave the sailor boys alone." So the last week of Cooper and Sally's Christmas vacation came to an end. Cooper left on Saturday to give himself a day to get ready for class.

Greta had an intense dislike of Cooper's truck. It's a 1933 Model A Ford truck with a bed. It was one very highly polished vehicle with a different engine.

The boys at Cal Poly, taking a mechanics course, completely over haul the machine and produce a whole new structure. The only items left as original are the cab and the bed.

Everything else in the vehicle is new or redone. The truck is painted a brilliant yellow and crimson red.

The headlights and taillights are modern. Every fall this Ford is overhauled as a students project.

# CHAPTER 7

Sally has been climbing up and down the stairs. Cooper is driving home from college. It is just a tad over 300 miles. Cooper is in a hurry as Sally is graduating from high school.

Cooper believes Sally, with her grades, should be, easily in the top ten percent of her graduating class.

Graduation is June 6 and these two leave two days later on Sally's fire engine red tandem bicycle.

As Cooper said at Christmas, "It is just an easy jaunt of about four hundred and two easy miles or so."

Then Sally asks, "Are you counting the engine in the back to do all the work? You said we'll have miles of hills before we get to the desert."

"Don't worry about it, many people have already bicycled this route we are taking without a problem, and I have also.

The high school graduation in San Diego was held outdoors in the football stadium.

Parents packed the seats. The graduates entered by two's. And they are seated in the north end zone.

Sally is wearing a sharp red dress and new red high heels, once Greta found out the grads would walk on a wooden sidewalk.

Greta, Jude, and Dr. McGill are thrilled as Sally walks past with her hand on her partner's elbow to the quickly built stage on the football field.

The graduating students are in front and on one side of the stage, opposite the school band. The stage holds the top ten percent and the the top school administrators and certain officials.

On the other side the school band is ready and the guests have bleachers along with portable bleachers, making the football field only 50 yards long.

Charley Chin, the Student Body President, sits in the end zone with the 10 percenters and administrators, and has an empty chair next to him. After everything has settled down, a prayer is given.

Everything is quiet. People are waiting. Charley Chin, The Student Body President stands up and walks to the ten percenters and stands in front of Sally.

He bends over and in a low voice he says to Sally. "It's me, Charley. Take my elbow."

"Why your elbow, Charley?" "You have the wrong seat."

These two have known each other since kindergarten. Charley escorts Sally to the empty seat next to him. Nothing more is said. There are some murmurs in the crowd.

Now the graduation begins. Then came short speeches from administrators, some public officials, and a congressman.

Charlie Wong, the Student Body President, gave his short speech regarding leaving high school and going out into a different world. This talk was accepted by the teachers committee.

During the graduation ceremonies and after Charlie finished his speech, there was loud clapping from the audience and the graduating class.

Charlie returns to his seat, but did not sit down. Then he reaches his hand down an takes Sally's arm quietly saying, "Stand up, Sally, we are going to the center of the stage. Yes, you and I. Take my elbow, now, let's go."

He leans over to a very surprised Sally and whispers, "We have known each other too long. My address to the students is about you.

Let's go gal, I have the stage, and finally you are going to receive the tribute you fully deserve."

Sally half whispers, "Charley, no one told me about this?" "Well, that's interesting. I guess they will know now." The teachers "on guard" around the stage were somewhat surprised, like a lot.

Dr. Robertson, the high school principal, sitting in the front row on the stage, gave a slight wave and a shake of his head to the worried teachers, as if to say, don't worry.

At the microphone Charley Chin held up his free hand as the other hand is gripped by Sally. He squeezes her hand indicating every thing is OK.

He tells Sally, "I'll be next to you, Sally. Here we are. Stand still, this speech is short."

Charley holds up his left hand as his right is holding Sally's left hand tightly. Smiling he speaks through the microphone, "Class, our teachers, our band, and our family and friends, it is my privilege, right, and pleasure to say to all of you: From our kindergarten days together and still friends and classmates. To me the bravest and greatest classmate ever, the conqueror of one tremendous problem who gave hope over all our minor ills and pains, is Sally. So, Sally, from all of us here, to the greatest person I've ever known may I request all of you here and out there to join in, showing our love to Sally Wilhelmina Portage Santana. Hit it gang. A roar of yells and applause rip through the athletic field. Dr. Richardson walks up to microphone and nods to the student band director, Dr. Aaron Goldberg.

Now the school band stands up and begins playing Robert Burns Scottish hymn, "Auld Lang Syne."

With the audience, students and surprised teachers, they all join in singing and crying, and led by Dr. Richardson. At the same time, Charley hands an extra handkerchief to Sally, saying "keep it close by, I may need it later."

Dr. Richardson speaks into the microphone, "Do it one more time. This time make it louder!"

After the second hymn, Charley and Sally are still standing. Charlie leans over to Sally, still holding her hand and whispers, "Sorry for not telling you, but give your classmates a few quick words, Sally."

Sally, standing with Charley, uses her left arm and makes a fist with her right hand; and shakes her fist at Charlie.

Now Sally speaks into the microphone, "One of these days, Charley Chin."

The crowd roars. Sally, still holding Charley's other hand, reaches for the microphone."

"If it weren't for my father, my mother, my eye doctor, my brother, and all you excellent teachers and all my classmates, I couldn't have done it. You have given me hope and help that allowed me to stretch the curriculum when eyesight was needed. None of you will ever really know how much you helped me.

"But I do, and sometime in the future I hope I can pay back your gracious assistance. I hope to return and pass on your help to similar students needing assistance. Charley, to my seat, please."

Again the band played, except this time Dr. Robertson, using his outstanding baritone voice, and facing Sally with his hand around her, along with the director of the school orchestra, restarted singing the Scottish hymn.

Then everyone stood up again singing the old hymn. More tears again rolled off faces from graduating students, friends and families. What a graduation it was.

Later in Jude's car, Jude, Terri, Greta, Cooper, and Sally all were dabbing their eyes. Sally kept saying, "That was not in our program. No one had the slightest idea Charley and the band, unless our music instructor Dr. Goldberg or Dr. Richardson came up with that idea. I cried a gallon of tears."

Jude comments, "You should have been in the audience Sally. I never saw or heard so much crying and that was everyone crying for you.

"Sally. You've have a life long project to pass on. And knowing you young lady, you will, any thoughts?"

"Dad. I haven't said this to anyone, I would like to be a clinical psychologist, if I'm able to tackle what I have to know without my vision."

Terri comes in. "With your challenges, I'm advising you to go straight through to your Doctorate. You'll need help on how to get started and I would be very unhappy, if you didn't use me."

Greta comments, "Excellent, I go along with your Father. When Charley caught the teachers off guard, he did so perfectly. Now you have college and swimming scholarships: You are going to USC, right?"

"Mom, you remember that I signed the papers." Terri mentions, "It's too soon for a major yet, but do you have an idea, Sally?" "Well I really hadn't zeroed in on one until this great graduation. I owe a lot to so many people. Yes, I'm going to major in some kind of psychology, including visual impairment like mine.

Terri opens up: "I want everyone to know, in this car, that I have not talked to Sally regarding a major in college. But you, young lady, you'll be a fantastic addition to Graduate studies. I'm thrilled with your college selection. If there is anything I can do to help just whistle."

After arriving home the telephone never seemed to be silent for a minute. Everyone, from the neighbors, school friends, and strangers were calling. The newspaper wants to set up a time, darn soon for a interview.

Jude finally took over the telephone calls. He informs the callers by saying, "You have two days to get on Miss Sally Wilhelmina's interview list.

"Where she is going, you asked? "She is leaving in three days with her brother on a bicycle ride where there are no phones or radios.

"Sally and her brother are taking this bicycle ride that's been promised over four years ago."

"Yes, yes, I understand your position. Sally's position also must be understood."

"Where they are going? If I tell you then it's not what Sally and her brother want. Thank you for calling, anyway, click."

Terri speaks up. "Jude, you should handle Sally's telephone calls. You're good with that. I would have told those people that it wasn't their "G D" business and slammed the phone down right on their ear."

"We went through that crap with the four kids regarding the poachers and the lost child. Now we have the same type of people and the same questions."

Terri continues. "Jude, how's your world business doing?" Jude looks over to Sally, Cooper, Greta, and Terri. Then he looks at his watch. "Oh, got to go."

Greta isn't smiling. Jude has a half smile. "May I see them off, Greta." "Why not? It's also your house Jude." "OK, all." He goes over to Cooper and hugs him. "See you in couple of days, about what time will you leave?" He receives a half smile from Cooper and a grunt. "Probably right after noon. The first night we will be at the state park in Encinitas, Dad." Jude nods, then reaches for Sally. He notices her eyes are red and watery. He kisses her. "You have a good leader, Sis. I'll be here, yeah, I'll see you two off Monday."

He looks at his frowning wife, "Monday, I'll stop by after lunch and see the kids off."

Finding no further response he bows to all, gives Terri a wink, and leaves from the front door, being very careful not to slam the door.

Terri gives Greta a stern look. She thinks Greta is going to say something. "Greta, lets go in the kitchen get dinner started. I have a night call later on at the hospital.

As the two ladies walk into the kitchen, Terri says to Greta, "No, please drop that subject right now. We'll talk about it next week. Don't bring the subject up you're thinking about. Lets get to work."

Greta starts to ask a question. Terri, almost whispers, "Hold it. we'll talk later, just you and me. Not now."

Late on Monday morning Cooper is gathering certain items such as tools, tire patches, one extra tire and tube and a couple of extra chain links, in case the chain acts up. He had written a list of what to take and has gone over and over it and finally satisfied, he's ready to start loading.

"Our bike ride," Cooper tells his father, "is around 400 miles and should take eight or nine days.

"This ride will depend on stops to visit some of the places missed in a car. It all depends on stops to see or experience something interesting as we bicycle to Yosemite National Park.

Coop mentions to his sister, "Remember Sally, our camping stops will depend on where the area looks good and safe. The earlier we rise in the morning then the less head winds we'll fight during the afternoons, and we won't have to make camp in the dark. So there's sleeping—in in the morning."

Sally looks at her brother. "Hmmm. I thought this long bike ride was a vacation for us, Coop?"

# CHAPTER 8

On Monday morning the house is awakened by a loud voice: "Come on Miss Portage, we've planned this trip for six months, so let's go."

The tall 17-year-old blond, who just graduated from high school with a scholarship to USC, snaps at her brother. "Don't worry, 'Coop.' I'm just about ready. You've been ranting around our house and yard for the last three hours. It's a girl's privilege to get prepared before going anywhere. "Sally, I've been telling you all this morning, we have to get started as we have miles to go and your lolligagging will drag us into camp at dark; and it's tough to set up camp in the dark and fix a meal." "Oh really? I've been going in the dark for eleven years but I'm not hard of hearing. So lower your voice or you'll get the neighbors upset as well as your sister."

Sally finishes running her hands around and over her bright yellow panniers that are hooked onto the fire engine red tandem bicycle.

"You just keep your jawing, big brother, and you'll be riding this tandem alone. Are Mom and Dad here? Can you see them?"

"Yeah, along with Terri." It is a bright warm Sunday morning and with the help of the sun, the fog is now burning off.

Just looking down Portola Avenue in San Diego, the street is lined with tall tulip trees. The flowering trees are now in full color displaying sulfur yellow and chartreuse flowers.

Standing on the verdant lawns are some of the neighbors of Greta and Jude Portage. They watch the brother and sister prepare for a bicycle ride to Yosemite National Park. They smile, as the brother and sister are finally ready for their long trip. The two have been practicing for two weeks riding all over San Diego this summer.

Off to one side stands Jude Portage, the four-year separated husband of Greta, and the father, of the two bicyclers. He's smiling.

Jude still manages a world wide systems software company. Greta, his ex-wife, has gone back to work.

She holds a position as a sales manager with a small silk flower company. Greta had to find something to do as her two young adults are growing up.

Jude cautions his two bicyclers: "Be careful you two, remember you're riding together for seven to ten days. Stay friends," came the soothing voice of their Father, as he tries to ease the beginning of tension between his two strong-headed young adults."

Jude reaches over and places his arm around Sally, bending over he gives his daughter a kiss on her cheek. "Take a deep breath, honey. Everything is loaded, tires pumped up, water on board, and it's a great sunny day. Your mother gave us all a great lunch. Your lunch should last until your campground on the beach."

"Dad, I'm really waiting for Doctor Terri. She wanted to see us off this morning. That's what she told me."

"I know that, however, she just called your Mother and something has come up. She promised your Mother she'll see you two in Yosemite when you arrive."

"You're not coming?" Slowly and quietly Jude replies, "No, I don't think so. I have a business problem right now. I have to get to work and I have a mile high pile of papers on my desk waiting for me.

"It's not Mom, is it?" "Don't worry about that item. Enjoy your ride and your brother will see to that." He turns to his frowning and mediating wife. "Greta, you'll meet the kids in Yosemite with Dr. Terri?" Greta nods. Another shake and a hug with Cooper, a wave to Greta, and Jude slowly walks away toward his car, passing his wife, "Greta, be sure to get the kids off as the afternoon winds will slow them along the beach trail."

Greta, with a tired slow answer says, "Why, of course I will, Jude. I'll make sure if one doesn't try to chop the other's head off before they leave."

Sally's hand reaches out and feels for her mother. Pulling her mother close she brings her Mother's head next to her mouth and whispers, "I just wish you and Dad would come to Yosemite as a family that we had once."

Greta whispers back, "I understand your thoughts, but Jude has a problem or two to solve. In a week or so, we'll see you two. Don't let that worry you.

"But I noticed, last night, you were tossing and turning in your bed most of the night. You have a problem I don't know about?"

Sally, still holding onto her Mother's head, quietly tells her, "I don't know. Well maybe. I've never had a dream like this one. I sure had a bad dream that something will happen to us on our bicycle ride. I'm half scared, Mom."

"Sally, honey, it's the excitement of this ride. So don't let this thought dwell on you. Why don't you keep that as a secret just between you and me.

"You know your brother will not let anything happen to you. You have the best brother any girl would want."

"OK, Mom, I know that too. But I sure wish you and Dad were going with us."

"I know and your brother tells me the same. However, it's our problem to work out so don't let that keep you from enjoying your bicycle ride."

Cooper walks up to the whispering two, and says, "OK, Sister Sally, I'm going. If you're going, get on. I'll hold the bike."

Cooper turns his head when passing girls while bicycling. Sally's brother is 22 years of age, tall, a 6'3' blond with blue eyes, and makes quite a picture when running, bicycling, and surfing.

He was an All American soccer player in college, a second string Little All American football player nearly finishing his Master's in architecture and has an engineering degree at California Polytechnic University in San Luis Obispo.

Cooper orders his sister, "You finally ready? I'm pushing off, little one."

"I'm not a little one, I'm 5'9. I'm just six inches shorter than you, big boy. Lets get this show on the road or do I pump it myself? What's wrong? Did that date, last night, with the flight attendant who had a squeaky voice, turn you down?"

"Easy back there, lady. You need my eyes. Speaking about eyes, your bicycling outfit is something else. Did Mom go with you to by those clothes?"

"Mom? No way. Dr. Terri McGill took me shopping and bought the whole outfit for my going away present."

"Sister Sally, you are some spectrum of color. Your sulfur yellow bicycling shorts seem as tight as can be. And your new socks the color of acid yellow, with the day glow saffron colored bicycling shoes sure clashes with your tight florescent yellow bicycling shirt, and your chrome white, tight bicycling shorts. "This combo certainly shows off your figure more than I think you should."

Sally smiles at her brother, She's thinking, I have packed away a red set and one set of pink shirts, shorts, and socks in the right pannier. I'm not biking in old maid subdued biking clothes. Cooper is slightly upset. He's thinking, I don't understand women, and especially the way men want to show off every line of their body. Yet, they become prudish when someone mentions it to them about how tight or revealing the clothes fit.

"Now my sister is wearing those tight biking shirts and shorts with her figure. Maybe it's not much different than wrapping herself in saran wrap.'

Sally smiles as she has heard brother's remarks before.

She is thinking, "He has no idea I have three more bicycling outfits out of sight in my rear right pannier."

"Wait till he sees them, especially the nude pink ones Dr. Terri had made for me.

Sally reaches around her bicycle handlebars and pulls on her bicycling helmet. She is smiling. "Wait till he sees this helmet. This will wind him up tight." Sally's helmet has special paint in the color of a ripe mango."

"Holy smokes, Miss Sally Wilhelmina Portage Santana. Your bicycling clothes, if that is what you call your ensemble, and now that painted helmet. It almost makes me want to throw up."

Sally came back with: "It doesn't bother me a bit. At least they can see me. Maybe they'll wonder why that "trampy" looking guy in front, I'm bicycling with, has such an outstanding young lady that really knows what to wear on the bike."

"Yeah, sister Sally, you're right. They will see your glow before any vehicle rounds the corner and sees us.

"It's good thing you didn't wear those clothes and that color when you were rounding those cattle on the McGill's ranch. We would still be chasing cattle clear to Kansas City."

"What's wrong with the colors?" "Well, Sally, drivers will see you miles ahead or before coming around a turn. Those colors, to my way of thinking, are as close to being obscene as to not wearing anything."

"Then, Coop, the girls you date must be from a nunnery." "Well, are they that pure? OK, ready for me to shove off, Color Bean?" Sally asks, "How do our flags look and will we have any problems with them standing straight up?" "They won't. Lets get started, and before we hit Torrey Pines grade, I'll check them again, mother hen." Brother and sister give their last wave as they begin their bike ride to Yosemite National Park.

Jude Portage has stayed back to watch the two on that red tandem disappear. With a handkerchief, he gives his nose and eyes a quick wipe. Turning round he sees his separated wife, Greta, doing the same. He decides to remain a bit longer.

"Well, Greta, above everything else, we do have two great kids, smart, and with pleasant manners. For what ever else, regardless of what we did in the past; we certainly raised two excellent young adults. For this we can be very proud of them and ourselves. Do you have time for coffee at Pat's Coffee Shop?"

Greta first impulse was to say no. Then, she says, "Just one cup or I'll be shaking the rest of the day.

"Wait a minute, Jude. Why don't you come over for dinner tonight as Terri will be here and the three of us can—just talk." "What may I bring?" "Anything, but not one of your girl friends."

"That's a low blow there, lady. I don't have any. My work had been too involved to have such an expensive hobby, and I'll try not to make up an answer to your remark.

"However, I do have some home made wine from Angelo's ranch just outside of Temecula. May I bring two bottles, one red and one white?"

He receives a nod from Greta. She's thinking, Jude just said, his work had been very involved. What does <u>that</u> mean?"

Jude turns to leave, and then he turns around and tells his ex-wife, "Thank you for the invite. See you tonight, seven OK?"

Greta nods again and watches Jude leave. Then she wonders, why did I make that stupid remark to him. I know he doesn't date and I'm sure he knows that I date.

But none of those guys come close to Jude even in his bad moments, but it gets me out of the house. Is he still with that world wide company?

Two people on a fire engine red tandem bicycle are pumping hard and climb slowly up through the back of La Jolla. Then, still climbing, they finally reach Torrey Pines Park, a golf course at the north side, and on the edge of San Diego's warm afternoon. "Are we there yet, Coop?"

"We just passed the parking lot of Black's Beach. You have been there. We did some body surfing."

"Yeah, as I remember, I was told I was the only person on the beach, except those junior high girls that always walked, wearing their nothing bathing suits as they looked at all the naked boys and men.

"That's the place. You were the only girl on the beach wearing a bathing suit."

"Yeah. It was Mom's orders, but not to you." "I imagine I was the only one on the beach in a bathing suit with a nude fellow.

"But the surf was good for body surfing. Yeah, body surfing nude. And there's no heavy board to pack around.

"Coop. Remember Jenny and Rita when they saw us surfing. You sure must have given an eye full showing them how to surf the breakers. They were still talking about that Sunday at Blacks, even at our graduation."

"When do we start down the hill?" "Not yet. But we will have a great down hill run providing I don't have to keep telling my sister, 'Stay off the brakes, please.' "So Let it roll buddy."

"How fast are we going, Leader?" Cooper slightly turns his head to answer Sally. "Sister, we are doing thirty miles per hour already and we now have a car packed with tourists in front of us and everybody is looking at the beach and water."

"Take the car on the right, isn't that why we have bike lanes?" "Yeah, but we have a family riding bicycles, ahead of us. It is going to be a little slower until we are able to pass them." "How soon before we get to Encinitas and stop for a hamburger, leader?" "We're not stopping. Our campground is just beyond Encinitas. I don't want you to get fat and I don't go for fat girls."

"It didn't bother you when we were with Dad and Mom in Death Valley and you remember I saw you that evening?"

"Really?" "No, just slightly. But I saw your date, faintly as she was trying to run away half dressed with one shoe on and trying to pull her clothes on where they belong.

"Don't worry. I didn't say a word to Mom or Dad about that episode." "Thanks. Anyway that was a far as I was able to go with her." Their conversations continue until Cooper announced: "Hey lady.

Elijah State Park is just ahead." With perspiration streaming down her face, Sally is thinking: "We have more hills and even mountains ahead of us and I'm sweating buckets already." "Say, big brother, do they have showers at this park?"

"They sure do. Do you think you'll need one? Listen sister, going up Torrey Pines I didn't think you were hardly pushing on your peddles. We have some real mountains ahead of us, especially Tioga Pass going into Yosemite."

"Coop. As I remember, isn't that on the back side of the eastern side of Yosemite?" Why are we going out of our way? I was told there are two entrances to Yosemite on the west side. Why can't we take one of those roads?"

"There are three roads and you wouldn't like any of them, Sally. My last ride to Yosemite was two years ago and the bike ride up to Mariposa was the worst climb I've ever been on.

Man-o-man, that mountain road was steep. I almost walked it in places. The other two, the west entrances have way too much traffic to enjoy bicycling."

"OK, brother, you're the leader. How far are we from our campground?"

"Close. Do you smell the ocean and hear he breakers?" "Yeah, faintly." "Sally, we have a very slight uphill and then we'll be at the campground where we have a reservations for camping. We may meet other bicyclers, touring."

"All I want to know is: Does the campground have showers and toilets?"

"They sure do. I'll find a lady for you, if you're wondering about that."

"It never entered my mind. I just knew you would handle that problem when ladies are around. How close are we. Coop?"

"To the ladies?" "No, lover boy. The campground?" "One hundred yards. We'll stop at this ranger station right here.

Climb off the bike, hold it for me and stay right here with no wandering. I'll check us in."

"Wandering? You know I can't see to wander, Coop." "Yeah, but sometimes you find ways." The ranger station is manned by a lady ranger. Cooper tells her, "Yes, one night for two. Are their other bicyclers already in?" "Three boys now and a family of four, not in yet, but they have reservations. You'll have plenty of room." Cooper signs in and then the Ranger mentions, "Your lady, out there, certainly has brilliant bicycle clothes. I think I could have seen her a mile away."

"That's my sister and she is almost blind. I promised her a bicycle ride three years ago, when she graduated from high school. She not only graduated but with honors and a double scholarship to USC." Not bad for a kid who soon will be completely blind."

"You mean your sister is blind? "Right on. She started when she was about six years old. Now she is 17 and in a couple of years she will be completely blind. She only sees light and darkness and shadows now. Maybe when she is in her twenties, she'll be completely blind."

"That is a sad thought for such a good-looking lady, when a dark world is ahead. Does she go to a school for the blind?"

"No way. She mainstreamed it right to the end in high school." "Was this in a private school?" "No way. My sister went all the way with our public schools. She had the best specialists with her every day. She had not only trained teachers but a teacher with her master's in Visual Impairment. One would say she did quite well. She was right in the top 10 percent of her class and has a academic and an athletic scholarship to USC."

Coop continues, appearing to be very proud of his sister, "I'm not saying this just because I'm her brother. Sally has accepted the fact that nothing can be done, mentally or physically.

My sister, from elementary school, prepared herself for the time when she would be completely blind. Losing her sight has been a gradual thing.

"Interesting." replies the ranger. "Does she have hobbies?" "She rides horses, and every two weeks in August she helps round up cattle on a ranch in Northern California. Once she was the best skier in our family. Now she skis with my Mother, Dad, or me skiing. One of the family is always beside her telling Sally what's ahead. She skis very slowly now." Coop continues: "Get this: My sister was a pitcher before her eye exam. She had to switch into another sport.

"She swam for four years on our high school varsity swimming team and always had the outside lane. Her coach would walk along side her and would blow a whistle if she began to veer left or right. And he used a different whistle when coaching her to make turns. She holds three high school national sprint records.

"Schoolwork is in braille now but she once used magnifying lenses on large print books. Computers for the blind are a great help for her but are very expensive.

"She eats up talking books. She's always listening to books of all kinds, fiction or non-fiction. We have three talking books with us, but I won't let her use her books while bicycling."

"Why?" "I may have to give a quick order, like putting on the brakes or to pick up the speed or we are stopping." "At home, in her room, she has one wall with blue ribbons of her swimming races. My sister won a four-year scholarship in swimming as well as academics to USC."

The ranger is surprised. "We have visitors coming here that are, may I say visually impaired?" "That's the term to use, but not around Sally. She claims, 'So I'm blind, but I'm not impaired. I'm also not the person that has to be in a carnival or circus."

Coop continues, "My sister always remarks. "I do have five other facets that make my life complete.

"I may not be able to see the person or the scene but I can mentally judge the person, or the scene, by tone, voice, words, smell or touch.

"What's left? Those you cannot fake, but the voice you can." "Good for her." Remarked the lady ranger. "May I come by your site, I'm due for a break and would love to talk to her as I meet many sightless people in this business. I could use some help on what I can do to for those people to make camping a more enjoyable experience."

"Knowing my sister, she would love to talk to you or anyone else. But be ready for her philosophy of life. Also, she will need a guide to go to the restroom and shower soon."

"I'll take her. Have a good evening and I'll be by for your sister in about ten minutes. Is that all right?"

"Perfect. "Wait, Mr. Portage. Is your sister the one I read about in the 'Union' about a graduation that had the crowd in tears as well as the graduation class?"

"That was my sister. When you take Sally into the rest room, ask her, she'll tell you her side of the story."

"Cooper and Sally's bicycle campsite is about the size of two normal camping areas. This site can hold ten bicycles or ten walkers, easy. When Sally and Cooper arrive three boys, as the ranger said, would be there.

The first thing Sally hears is a whistle. So she gave the boys a big smile and a wave. It was not quite exactly where the boys were sitting. They laugh.

Coop" stops the bicycle and lets Sally off. Then quietly mentions to Sally, "Your wave missed the boys by 45 degrees. Make a half right turn wave to them again."

Sally turns. "Sorry boys, I missed you with my wave. These are cheap glasses."

One of the boys says loudly, "I don't care where you look you still look great. Where are you two bicycling?"

"Yosemite National Park." replies Sally. "That's some distance." Sally is leaning on the tandem talking to the three boys while Cooper works. He strips the tandem bicycle of their panniers, tent, and sleeping bags.

Then he places Sally on a picnic bench seat takes the tandem and leans the bicycle against the fence and locks the tandem to the fence. One other bicycle is locked to the fence.

Sally, now standing, is talking to a tall blond lad.

Cooper walks up to her, as she is still talking, and pokes her with his right elbow. "It's tent fixing time, lady."

"Coop, this is Eduard Bruner. That's his bicycle locked on the fence. Cooper shakes hands with Eduard Bruner. Eduard asks, "Let me help you with your tent. One of the boys has a similar tent, Cooper." "I appreciate your offer, but Sally and I have practiced how to set up and take down." Sally suggests, "Eduard was telling me his camping experiences. Why don't we let the two boys see how fast they can set up a tent?" Eduard, replies, "I think they might, but with no directions, probably you will do nothing under ten minutes." Cooper is smiling, "OK, Eduard, I'll get the tent out and I'll time them.

Oh, for your information, Sally and I have put this tent, including the rain fly, on as well. Sally, what was our best time; four minutes and 30 seconds, correct?"

"Correct, and not timed by me if you thought differently, Eduard." Coop continues, "I would say with those two green horns, you mentioned Eduard, the ones that can't put their bikes away, no way. Putting up a tent," maybe 40 minutes?""

One of the boys said, "Get the tent over here and time us. We don't need Eduard. You only have one and a half people and we have two good campers."

Cooper brings the tent out, unlatches the holding bundle of tent needs. Then Cooper says, "OK gang. I'll time you. Start."

Cooper suggests, "OK, under fifteen minutes. When do you want to start?"

Two of the boys, together said, "Start the clock." Coop moves Sally over to the table and benches, saying, "We'll watch them from here. The tablecloth is next to you and dishes and cups are out in front of you. Sally, let's see how quick we can set a table?"

The two boys are having a problem deciding which rod goes where on the inside tent. There are four long rods and two short rods.

Cooper had taped a number on each rod and a number on the tent.

Sally says to Eduard, "I'll bet they can't do it faster than we. We practiced about, well it seemed, a hundred times.

"What was our best time, Coop? Four and half minutes, was that time correct?"

"You're right, Sally, it was four and half minutes." The two give up. Sally laughs. Let's show these two boys what you can do under a half hour." Cooper guides Sally around the table and places the tent out. "OK Sally like we did at home. One of you boys have a watch, time us." Every part of the tent, the ground cloth, tent, poles and stakes are on the ground. "Sally, are you ready?"

"Lets go, Coop." One of the boys who is timing with his wrist watch yells out, "Six minutes and they got the tent is up and the rain fly is on. Wow!" As Cooper hammers in the last peg and the tent is stiff and ready for the night. Then he guides Sally over to where the boys are standing. "Lads this is my sister, Sally, and she is blind. But this little loss doesn't stop her except steering a vehicle, walking alone or bicycling."

All that came out of the boy's mouths was "Wow" or "Holy cow." Cooper laughs as the shocked look came from the boys. Then he asks,

"Where are you lads headed?"

One boy, a good-looking barrel chested lad, who had been talking to Sally replies, "We are headed to Los Angeles. I'm in my second year at USC and Burt will be a freshman. The blond guy will be in UCLA for what reason I don't know."

Cooper asks the speaker. "Are you on a swimming scholarship? "Yes, but how did you know it?" "Your chest. Maybe you'll see Sally, that's where she's headed and also with a swimming scholarship. Watch out for her, she'll drown you just swimming over you.""Coop, that's not a nice thing to say."

Eduard snaps out. "Holy Smokes. This is really, it's you, uh, Sally. I heard about you two weeks ago when I made a quick trip to college to correct something in my records.

"My swimming coach told me, "We have a blind girl coming that can swim circles around our girls and even you, Eduard.

"She's going to make every swimmer work harder and she is blind. We think she'll tear up some records."

This big lad continues, "Then, it's really you I heard about? Our whole swimming department is all in smiles?

"Gee, I don't know about the records Eduard, but I'm going to USC on a swimming scholarship." Replies Sally.

This barrel chested stranger says, "Excuse my ignorance, my name is Eduard Bruner." Cooper asks, "Sounds German. Is it?" "Sure is, is that a problem?"

"Not at all, "We are half Mexican. Sally and I are first generation in the mix for all that means. It's not much to us. Our last name is Portage Santana.

Eduard smiles. "We have the same thoughts here. I have two younger brothers and one seventeen year old sister that can hardly wait to graduate from high school, and go to some college somewhere at the end the world, anywhere just to be away from home. You know, our whole family can hardly wait for that time."

"Mom is staying home until everyone, but Dad, leaves. Then she keeps telling the family. "When everyone is off to college, Then I'll go back to the lab, or to teach, somewhere, where life is peaceful again."

Sally is smiling and she says, "Eduard, I'll be looking for you when I enter USC. Well looking for you, that's not right, maybe I'll be hearing about you. My first name is Samantha, but I go by Sally, Why, I don't know. My last name is Portage Santana. "Like Coop. I'm half Mexican. Mom is English, Scot, Irish, and perhaps a touch of German. I'm just a typical American. It's not the bloodline, but who you are that counts.

"In our family, Eduard, we aren't breeding dogs and horses, so who cares what your blood line is or what you think you have. That's the end of my sermon."

Sally taps her brother's arm. "Coop, I have to clean up. Can you grab my right pannier, the one that has the red bow on it and hand it to me? This girl needs to be clean and smell nice, hint hint to you, brother. Also, my cane, please. Save some dinner for me."

Cooper hands Sally the pannier and her cane and they start to leave when the lady ranger arrives.

Then Coop introduces Sally to Lori, the lady ranger. Lori tells Cooper, "Let me handle this. I need to know exactly how this is done, OK, with you?"

Sally suggests, "Certainly, it's better than having a man wait as he cracks his knuckles then checks and rechecks his watch waiting for a lady."

Sally then tells Lori, the Ranger, "We'll start lesson one now. We start by letting me have your elbow. I'll teach you how to do sighted guide. It's not hard but different from guiding your maiden aunt." And off the two ladies went.

Eduard comes up to Cooper. "When I was talking to Sally, she had her dark glasses on and I never picked up that Sally is blind. What a beautiful and smart sister you have. I assume you are going to college?"

"Thanks for your nice observations, Eduard. I'm at Cal Poly at San Luis Obispo in a Master's program. My major was Architecture with a minor in Engineering. I am planning to do a couple more years of engineering. I'd rather work on buildings than houses, and you?"

"Well, Coop, I've finished my second year and had to make my choice. I'm leaning toward law. I've taken enough classes to make a number of choices. Law was what I selected in February.

"I'd combine that with another major to be more knowledgable when I go to court knowing something more about people than just law." "So I'm thinking of a double major and finally signed up in Sociology.

I just think it might help in law. And does Sally have any set goals, Cooper?"

"She's talking about going into Clinical Psychology and work with elementary school class problems. She can handle that being blind. Getting around may be problem. But she has at least four years to figure that minor situation."

Cooper and Eduard are in deep conversation when Sally returns with the ranger. She says to the group. "Smell me. After dinner I want each and every one of you guys to smell like anything except the perspiration of clothes or bodies or the combination of both, as you do now. I don't want to go to sleep thinking I'm in a stall with goats, cows, pigs and horses."

One of the young boys popped up, "I just had a shower last night. Why tonight?"

Sally snaps. "Because there's a girl present. You do not need another reason."

"OK, OK, I'll take a shower. Just for you, even if you're going to USC." "You're learning, but I don't give you much hope right now."

Eduard tells this two friends, "Sally is right, let's get a shower and bring your own soap and your own towels." The boys leave.

Lori, the female ranger, is sitting at the table, laughing. Then she asks, "Could you, Sally, just fill me in on your eyesight problem. Just watching you in the women's rest room, with your cane and without my help, I'm impressed."

"OK, Lori, people ask me any questions and I've heard them before." "If it bothers you, don't talk about it." "Hey Lori, that sentence is one of many that bothers me. Here goes.

Correct me Coop, if I miss something." Sally begins. "When I was about ten or twelve years old with big brother, I tried to do what ever he could do. I was a first class pest, right "Coop?" "It's not exactly the word I would use or had used at one time. Go a head Sally." Sally turns toward Cooper and smiles at her big brother. "Well, anyway we played catch with his baseball. When I was much younger, I was on a tiny tot baseball team. All my teammates did was to stand and look at balls going past them.

Then they might remember to stick their glove up to catch the ball but more likely to protect them from being hit. If they were lucky, they might catch or trap a ball.

"A few times they threw the ball and it was any one's guess where it was going to go. So I, at five years of age or younger, would play catch with Cooper.

"At six or seven I began to have some problems seeing the ball and would go running to my mother crying that my big brother was or is trying to hurt me. I was having trouble seeing the easy lobs he tossed to me.

"This problem began to happen more and more especially around dusk. In the house, before all the lights were on, I would walk into a wall or chair.

"We have, now, a family friend who is an ophthalmologist. Mom called Dr. Terri McGill and then we went to see her. What I have is something called R.O.P. or Retinopathy of Prematurity.

"Which means, in my later youth or maybe somewhere in my twenties, I will be completely blind. I might see shadows. Right now I'm eighteen years old, and seeing some light and darkness and some cloudy movements. But for all practical purposes, I'm blind."

Ranger Lori asks Sally, "While I was watching you in the rest room you seemed to handle your vision problem better than I've seen or anyone I know. How come?"

"Of course, Lori, it's my family and Doctor Terri. She beat into my thick skull this thought. "Don't let ever let this eye problem hinder you at all. There is nothing wrong with you except you have a vision problem. You can ski, ride a tandem bicycle, you swim and you are darn good at that, and you ride horses on my ranch. Get this: My brother made a mountain climber out of me.

With his friends, while Coop is in college, I still mountain climb. "One climber is always in the front and usually on belay. Behind me is another climber who also had me on belay. Finally, I learned to trust my partners

They would give suggestions and it worked great. Only one problem, there are no views for me.

"Sally," Coop interjects, "Remember last summer during our early fall roundup at Dr. Terri's ranch. You and I rode drag" We rode six days in the dust and you did your job as a darn good dragger. You were one of the best.

"The other cowboys thought you were great, and darn independent. They loved you Sally."

Sally continues, "Please don't lay it on so thick, Coop. So I followed Dr. Terri's advice and my parents and, of course, my closest friend, my big brother. We go every August on Dr. Terri's ranch for the roundup.

"Her foreman, Angelo Bonelli, a real nice guy, said to me, after last year's roundup was over. "Sally, gal, you ain't gonna get no more slack from us, sister. From now on you'll be treated like just like any other hands riding drag. Damn, you're good to have around."

# CHAPTER 9

JUDE ARRIVES AT 7 pm, for the promised dinner with Greta and Dr. Terri McGill. They are seated in the living room talking.

Jude is carrying a sack with two bottles of the white and red wine he promised to bring.

"Well, Jude." came Dr. Terri's voice, "You're right on time. We have the glasses ready. My day was a mess and Greta's day was full of worries. I think my phone rang six times with Greta asking me where the kids would be now on their bicycle ride. So I was the backstop since you were out of phone reach or ducking the phone completely."

Jude smiles. "Sorry, I can't agree with that, but I have been locked in our resource area going over a very sensitive project with my two top engineers. Eight hours later we finally found the problem.

"Now! I imagine the kids have already set up camp and knowing those two, they have already found new friends camping. Don't worry about them, they'll make it; the way those two gather acquaintances is like politicians running for election."

Jude looks at his ex-wife. "So, your day was also tough?" With large sigh, Greta replies, "It looks like, well two of us, this day for us isn't one to be proud of. One of these days I'm walking out from that company without even saying goodbye or maybe after telling them where they can stuff their company where sun never shines.

"Those people are something. What about you Terri? You look like you also picked up a problem? You haven't said a thing except mentioning my phone calls."

Terri looks over to Jude, "Can you bring us three glasses of that home made wine, red or white. please? I have a problem I'd like to share with you two. Are we close to dinner, Greta?"

"No. In a half hour. It's not a fancy dinner. No problem." Dr. Terry rearranges herself and begins. "I have been wrestling with this case for some time. Now I've come to two friends for help. "I have a six year old patient and her family is in the same position you two were eleven years ago, when we three found out about Sally. This morning I found out my patient will go through same physical and visual problems Sally went through and did a sparkling job."

Two voices almost together said: "Retinopathy of Prematurity, ROP?" "Exactly. It is almost the same situation you two went through. Damn it! They are starting down that, uh, well that road you two are traveling. Gang, I need your help.

"It's almost like they have a carbon copy of your actions when I gave you the word. They responded exactly the same.

"I need you two to meet these people and try to steer them away from the pitfalls you discovered. Can you help me?" Jude, immediately stood up. "Count me in Terri. I sure can tell them from a father's view point." Greta begins to mention, "Wait a minute, Jude, your work efforts started the split."

"No Greta, that's not entirely true. It took two of us to do it. If one were to make it into an equation, we failed. You were on one end and I was on the other end."

Dr. Terri raises both hands, "Recess time. Let me in this ring. Medical books devote pages on the subject and it's about all the same.

"Divorces are prevalent in situations like this. I don't want this one to turnout the same. Now friends, let me talk."

Dr. Terri McGill sits up, takes a steep swallow of her wine, nods to Jude and begins. "I want you two to come to my office on Tuesday at three in the afternoon. Just walk in as if you have an appointment. I will have this father, mother, and daughter in the waiting room. There will be no one else there and my office gal will take a break after fixing the telephones to be on the busy side."

Terri is now smiling. "Strike up a conversation with the family. Got it! Of course you have a daughter with ROP and tell them what has happened in the last eleven years.

"Warn them about differences between mother and father thoughts and listening to people that truly wanted to help you, but had no way to intelligently help you two.

"Why? Because no one, you knew, or anyone you talked to had gone through this problem or worse, even knew about. "Now, drag in your heavy artillery. Tell them your personal life problems. Tell them about the results of your stumbling and bumbling eventually with a four or six year separation which neither one of you wanted, but you did over all of my warnings.

"Tell them, you two just screwed it up. Eventually it worked out for the best, almost. Praise highly, your daughter who battled this problem and did a hell of a better job than you two did, in the beginning years.

"Tell them the only other person that responded correctly was your son, Cooper. "Tell them the truth. Your son did not let his sister become an invalid. Now, promise to stay current with them every day or night.

Terry is smiling. "You two, I don't care what house for dinner you use, but you want stay current with them and have them over when the slightest problem shows up. Can you do it for them, the girl, or even yourselves and how about me?

"I could have done a better overall job. I got those damn degrees on my wall showing off my medical skills. They could have worked better if hung them up in my garage. Will we work this out together?

It was quiet in the house for almost a minute. Terri is watching each face. Jude looks at his ex-wife. Then smiles and mentions, "I can do it. Boy, do I know the shock of being alone. I know my tears, my frustrations, and I know the barriers thrown up from friends I thought I once had.

"I know every bad advice I received on how to handle the problem with Sally and our own personal lives.

"Then I'll tell them how our daughter and our son survived a hell of lot better than Greta or myself. I've been down that damn road.

"I know those potholes and I can sure steer this couple away from some of those jackass problems that caught me.

And perhaps I can help them if a new problem arises. What we, Greta and I went through, no one else should have to do it. Count me in, Terry." Greta stands up and walks over to Jude. She grabs his face with both hands and gives him a real kiss. Looking at her nearly ex-husband in the eyes, she tells him, "Throw your date book away with mine. I'm going to be with you and you only, forever, starting tonight."

Terri jumps up and grabs the two with her arms, tears rushing down her face and with her voice cracking, "This I didn't expect but, I will accept it. Your darn rights I'll accept it. And accept it in trumps that is.

"Pour us more wine, Jude, and lets have dinner. Hell, this is a reconciliation dinner. Hot damn, my best friends are back together,"

During one very happy dinner, Dr. Terri always claims, home made wine should always be served in water glasses to appreciate the true bouquet and not be intimidated by fancy crystal goblets.

"Tell you what, gang, now the birds are nearly out of their nest, what are your plans for the future besides being back together, forever?"

Jude studies Dr. Terri carefully. He nods his head and answers: "I've been meaning to talk to you two about what's coming about a new company with two 'cracker jack' engineers. It's interesting they have the same feeling I have.

"Wait. I wasn't ready to open up this subject, but now I will." Jude turns to Greta, "Did Cooper tell you I saw him a couple of times in his school's coffee shop some six or eight months ago? "Yes. He was certainly surprised. Also, he enjoyed those dinners and long talks with you." "I've been talking to Coop a number of times in San Luis Obispo.

There are two instructors at Poly, that will be advisors for us before we get started and hopefully after we get started. Then we'll see if they will stay as consultants or work for us.

"When they found out our boy was the one that kicked the footballs and soccer balls, I would say they were impressed."

Smiling at both ladies, Jude continues, "My two engineer friends and I had an idea of making an electronic machine and will leave it alone as of now.

"With our idea we hope to increase the learning curve with every elementary school child that is struggling. This will allow teachers more time to work with each student.

"We have been working on this project for, well, forever, in the evenings in Robert Hunter's kitchen, Greta. Many times, you thought I was traveling. This project was not on company time.

This has been my mistress as well as theirs. These men, too, suffered very shaky marriages. We couldn't tell a soul as we didn't think it would fly like we hoped it would. Right now it appears to be a rocket.

All of our work as been done on our own time. From evenings and weekends sometimes, and more than a few times, almost to daylight.

"In fact, tonight those two men are taking their wives out to dinner to a very fancy place, I guess the fanciest in San Diego, with a private dinning room, just to tell them we are starting up a new business. Today we were told that it has been secured with a "million" patents.

"Our bank is coming in with us. Today was our last day in the old company. Our new building is a garage and will be available in 20 days. "The three of us will be taking our last company vacations starting now. Greta, Terri, lets catch the kids in Yosemite. I'll call the hotel and reserve another room."

During dinner, there were conversations certainly not planned, laughter, and still tears. This time tears of happiness. Jude looks at his wife and smiles. "Greta, you've had many ideas about a teaching tool and you've talked about it numerous times in the past. Would you care to join us in a non-paying job?

"Also, Terri, we may need your imput." Terri is smiling and tears come to her eyes. "Jude, I see things young kids should have. I'm far from being even close to a first year engineering student. I have a number of ideas that I would like to see done. You better get ready with my ideas."

Greta grabs Jude and tells him, "Honey, and I have wanted to say to you so many times that I'm going to be your unpaid partner, forever. And my tour starts tonight.

"You'll move your stuff, under my inspections, of course, tomorrow morning. Hmmm, lets make it early this afternoon. We'll use Cooper's old pickup. Tomorrow we'll get the rest of your stuff.

Terri stands up, "Hot damn. This is one evening I'll never forget." She tells Jude and Greta, "A toast to the best people I have ever had and to a new, make it, two new adventures. Both of you are back. Oh, Jude, you know you have another unpaid expert. I have cultured an idea for years to be used in my business."

Jude holds his water glass of wine high and adds, "First let me say to Terri. I've always had the feeling you have had your hand in getting us together for some time. No wonder you make your real money selling horses, you old horse trader. "Now to my two girls, one who just joined unpaid and one who will get all my money, thankfully again. I love you both."

More kisses go around the table. "If I know our kids and I'm sure Greta will agree, we will make a wonderful boy and girl very happy." Greta stands up with her glass of wine, tears running down her face, she adds, "To the cook, the ex-bride and to be the new bride who has always loved her mysterious traveling husband.

Greta replies. "The cook suggests dinner is ready. Thank you, Terri, for getting us all together. Tonight we have a well-cooked dinner and I now promise my new/old husband, this will be his last over cooked meal he will ever have."

"Two voices ring out in the living room. "I won't ever bet or drink to that promise. "But won't our two bicyclers be surprised."

# CHAPTER 10

ONE LONG, HOT 15 miles with a climb to reach Torrey Pines Park, right on the northwest edge of the city of San Diego.

It's a warm day with a great down hill run and Sally keeps telling Cooper, "Please stay off the breaks, Coop." "We can't, Captain, as we have some tourist using the bike lane with their car. Ahead of the car is a family, I guess, of five people all riding rentals going from the outside lane to the bike lane and back. We are almost to the bottom then we can hit it."

"How far to the campground and it better have toilets?" It has the full nine yards. We have about one mile to go. I'll check us in, first. Can you smell the water? Now don't try wandering around. We are about 100 yards above the beach. Can you smell the ocean?"

"I'd rather smell our campground.' "OK, Sally. I'm turning in and will stop now at the office." Inside the office is a lady California Ranger. Cooper tells the ranger,

"One night for two. Are their any other bicyclers in?" "Yes three boys. A family of four phoned but have arrived. Outside three other bicyclers you have a pick of spots as they have not paid or signed in."

Cooper pays and signs in.

The ranger is looking where the tandem is parked with Sally waiting for Cooper.

"Your lady by that red Tandem certainly has brilliant bicycling clothes on?"

Cooper takes quick glance. "She has. We received many toots from many cars. She has no idea how she looks. My sister s blind."

"Oh no. I'm sorry, I should not have asked."

"No problem. My sister Sally always remarks, 'I do have five other facets that make my life complete. I may not be able to see the person or the scene but I can mentally judge the person or the scene, by the voice tone, words used, and smell and touch.' "Then Sally always asks, 'whats left?'"

"Good for her," remarks the ranger. "May I come to your site, I'm due for a break and would love to talk to her. How long has your sister been blind?"

"Her blindness began when she was about in the sixth grade. She played baseball kept missing some catches. A year or two later, Mom took Sally to a eye specialist. My sister was getting blind and their is no cure.

"I had promised my sister a bicycle trip to Yosemite National Park when she graduated from high school with honors four days ago."

"Wait a minute! Was that the graduation I read in the 'Union' how everyone sang that a Scottish song, a hymn, I believe during graduation. And no one knew anything about it except a few. When I read the story I cried as well, and that's her out by that red tandem bicycle?"

"That's my Sally."

"Yes. From the paper it said. And the school Principal's voice was terrific. And the band and the Student President with the Principal along with Student Body President are the only ones that knew about your sister.

"And you are her brother and you didn't know about it?" Cooper enjoyed telling about graduation. "Not a hint. Charley Kwan, The Student Body President, said it was his idea. So he talked to the principal. We found out later, their principal was quite a singer in college and has sung opera in San Diego".

"What really hit the whole audience was when they repeated the Scottish hymn. Those that didn't have enough tears the first time had more when they sang it again." "If I wasn't mistaken," The ranger said, "According to the paper there was not a dry eye of all attending parents including the band, teachers, and the guests. Is that right?"

"Exactly. In school she was loved by everyone." "The paper mentioned her swimming." "Sally has broken two of the three high school sprint swimming records. She is a constant happy girl until race time and then speaks to no one. Her mind is going over the race, stroke by stroke, and what exactly she will do during the race.

"The non-talking includes her coach. He said to me, 'If your sister doesn't want to talk to me for a week before the race and always wins, I'm for it.'"

"After the race Sally is Miss Personality. May I suggest, would you be able to take Sally to the rest room for me?"

"Love to. I'd better find out this now. This is beginning my first year. I know this will come up again. I have a break in ten minutes. So, I'll be at your camp ground in ten minutes. Is that OK?

"No problem. I'm sure she would appreciate it. See you."

Cooper and Sally push their Red Tandem bike to their campground. Two bicycles are somewhat scattered around this camp. One bicycle is locked to the divided standard fence. Cooper tells Sally, "At least someone understands bicycling camping.""What do you mean by that remark, Coop?"

"There are three bicyclers and two bikes are just laying on the ground. One bike is cabled to a standard fence for security and out of the way. The other two bikes appear to trap-dropped like the owner appears not to give a, uh, heck."

Cooper is thinking, "a night call and some one will have, at least, two traps to stumble over."

While Cooper was chatting with Sally, three heads poke out of the other tent. The first words were, Ok, you two, I told you to pick up your bicycles and lock them next to mine. Get a move on it, we have guests." Sally says, "I'm not walking one foot alone you'd better have a flashlight with you if your taking me in the dark. That's your job. Well Coop all types of people camp."

Cooper mentions to Sally, "This campground appears to hold ten campers easy. I'll lead you to a bench and stay put while I take care of our panniers." A cool early evening breeze comes off the ocean and onto Eligo State Park Campground. It's sweater time as the temperature drops a few degrees.

Out of the other tent a tall barrel chested blond lad walks over to where Sally is sitting. He eyes Cooper getting ready to set up their tent.

This young fellow barks out, "You two guys were told to put your bicycle next to the fence and chain them to the fence; up and get it done now."

He shakes his head. "We are bicycling to the college they will be attending this fall if they don't kill them selves before we get there. Oh, my name is Eduard Brunner."

Cooper starts his introduction: "This is my sister, Samantha, she likes the name Sally better, and the last name is Portage Santana."

I'm Cooper, her brother. They shake hands." Eduard asks "Where are you headed?" Sally still wearing her dark glasses, jumps in. "My brother and I are bicycling to Yosemite. We live in San Diego, and you Eduard?"

"Sacramento. We are headed to Los Angeles but we wanted to see San Diego first. "We hear you have great weather. Right." Cooper adds "Always. Sally will be going to USC this fall on an academic and four year athletic scholarship." Eduard turns to Sally. And an athletic scholarship? What sport, Sally or is it Samantha?

"It's Sally. I'm a swimmer. I'm blind," "Then you are the girl they were talking about. I had to drive to USC to straighten some records three weeks ago. "I stopped into one of the offices. They told me, about, a highly intelligent and charming blue eyed blond girl that holds three National high school swimming records."

Sally has a small wok with some oil and is adding a couple of cloves of garlic.

Her second stove, a small stove, is heating precooked rice. Cooper adds some fresh garlic to the hot oil in his wok and waits. His second stove is now boiling the rice. The two soon-to-be college boys look out of their tent and begin to sniff like two Labradors on a quail hunt. This is the remark Cooper loves to receive. "Whatch you got to cook?"

Cooper's early bicycle trips, solo, have always ended with new friends amazed at his cooking and tonight is no exception.

These two boys dig around and bring what they were going to cook. Eduardo is still sitting next to Sally and she is smiling.

Into the wok everything went and the food is right up to the brim. Cooper stirs the wok as it starts to boil. Then he turns the burner down to a simmer.

Sally sits on the table bench still talking to Eduardo. Her hand is rubbing on the tablecloth Cooper carries with him. "What am I feeling under the table cloth, Eduard?"

Eduard replies. "Some idiot or two had to carve their initials into the wood top. Just some dumb stunt to attract attention to other air heads." "You mean all the ridges I feel are from someone carving on the table?"

"Probably more than one demented person did the job. We have to share space with these people."

"You mean, every table that Coop and I will camp by will have their carvings on tables?"

"Yep, most, and everything else they can screw-up in the environment. Not everyone is a good camper. Sorry to say that but it's true. Cooper, is that true in camping?"

Cooper replies. "Sally, Eduard is correct. I've seen even rocks chipped, while mountain climbing, with some ones initials."

Then Cooper hollers out. "Dinner's ready gang. Grab your plates and let's get it before it becomes cold."

Sally is thinking, I think that being blind has some attributes. At least I don't have to see our environment wrecked. But when biking, I sure can smell some of the garbage people leave or toss out the car window.

"One of the boys asked Cooper a question he has always been asked, "What do you call that mixture you have in your wok, Cooper?"

Sally has waited for that question, she answers, "My brother calls it slumgullion."

Eduard, still setting next to Sally, mentions, "It's the same as the one dish Mom has for us at home.

"Our whole family tries to figure out what's in the dish. Mom never tells except to say. "Eat it up. Many people are starving in the world."

"Eduard, how do you like my brother's cooking?" Sally quizzes Eduard. "I have to say it is as good or a trifle better than Mom's. Is there any chance we can get him to USC as a our cook?" "What do you mean, our cook, Eduard?" "Wow, just a term Sally. Cafeteria cooking is good but a change, at times, would be better." "Mr. USC, have you ever thought of eating out occasionally?" "A time or two but eating out is expensive, Sally. During swimming time we have access to the training table. You'll like it. Every dinner is different and much better than our cafeteria cooking."

"You mean we will eat somewhere else during swimming time?" "I'm told, Sally, this year, all athletics on teams, will be able to have dinner during school at the training table and it is in a special building. "You are on a scholarship, Sally, so you'll be in on the dinners. Sally's mind is clicking. I kinda like this guy. He sounds mature not like those kids with him. Just play your cards smart lady.

Dinner is over and the three boys and Cooper take the pots and dishes and utensils to the washroom. While they are gone Sally goes over her conversation with Eduard.

His voice sounds great and his manners are a lot better that the other two boys. I could hear them eating and banging their eating utensils. Well, at least I'll know one person when I go to college.

In the morning, Cooper and Sally are having breakfast. Silently they have taken down their tent and are nearly packed up before the three boys show their heads out from their tents.

Pot washing is over and Eduard comes over to the table and sits next to Sally. He asks," Where are you two going tomorrow?"

Sally touches Edward on his arm and says, "I'm just the engine. Talk to the conductor."

Cooper answers. "OK, lady, remember that as tomorrow we begin the hills and mountains. We are having just a short trip to Doheny State Beach Campground. We'll go through the US Marine Station at Camp Pendleton."

Eduard looks at Sally's second bicycling clothes. "Hmmm, with what you're wearing, Sally, that should alert those Marines. Wow, this morning you have even more colorful bike clothes than yesterday. I wish I were going with you two even if it were just to see what you'll wear tomorrow."

Sally replies. "Now, now, don't get all excited. I dress like this so people in cars or trucks will be sure to see two bicyclers."

"Sally, they'll see you before they come around the turn in the road." answers Eduard." "You mean the girls don't dress like this at your campus?" "Some do. Before you two leave, may I give you my telephone number? I want to make sure, are you planning to join a sorority?" "What made you ask a silly question like that, Eduard? I want a good quiet dorm with all girls." "I was hoping you'd say that, Sally. Would I be so bold as to say, I know a couple or three dorms you would love to live in. They run a tight ship, meaning they have enjoyable fun, but grades come first."

"With you being a man, how would know about that? Is that where you get your girl friends?"

"No, quick mind, But I do know some of the girls that live in these dorms. Most of them are in athletics and they do study."

Then Eduard touches Sally's hand and hands her a slip of paper. "Here is my name, and my address and telephone number. At some time during a break in school or projects we're both in, may I take you to dinner where they have candles and quiet music? I promise I'll have you home way before curfew and I won't carve my initials on the table."

Sally and even Cooper are surprised. Cooper had a sudden liking to this young lad. Eduard's eyes never left Sally's face. Any other boy would be giving her figure a long careful look.

Cooper considers Eduard more of a student and not going to college just to have fun. Besides he's been there for a year and knows the territory.

"Eduard, I can't speak for Sally but that is a nice offer." Sally speaks up. "Thank you big brother for your assistance in my new life away from home." Eduard, I'll call you when

Mom takes me to college. I'll phone you, then, and perhaps we'll find a nice dorm. I don't need a lot of help, but some help."

"I have one last question, Sally." "Last question now or forever?" "Now. "Will you be having dog with you?" "I don't think so. Is that correct Coop?"

Cooper replies. "As far as I know a dog is in the future and you'll have to spend time training with a dog."

Cooper continues, "I do know it's in the future. What I'm concerned about now, Eduard, is how Sally is going to get to her classes, dorm, and just get around the campus on normal class days?"

"No problem, Coop. Our university has a department for disabled students and students are assigned to assist all types of impaired persons; did I say that right, Sally?

Sally slips in, "Eduard, you are one fast learner. I have a feeling I'm going to have a step-brother watching me in college."

Eduard touches Sally's hand again, "All I want to happen is that you, Sally, will receive a lot of help. That's why I would like you to be with a group of caring girls and not that society bunch of party girls. We do have a bunch of "sniffers" and drinkers and they usually last only for one or two years of school."

Eduard stands, pats Sally on the back of her classy bike shirt, "Well, I'm packed up and ready to go. Good luck, Sally, on your trip and I'll make it a point to see you at USC."

Cooper places his hand on Eduard's back. "I'll walk with you to your bike."

While the two boys slowly walk out of Sally's hearing, Cooper tells Eduard, "Thank you for your help with Sally. I've been her watchdog for many years. Now she is going away into an environment that will be beyond what many sighted people fail to navigate through."

"You're right, Coop. I've seen the start and end of physical and mental breakdowns all the way through the schools I've gone to. Well, Coop, I'm sure we'll meet again. Have a good bicycle ride. I wish I were going in your direction."

Lets keep in touch, maybe we can even get a bicycle ride next summer with Sally and some one else.

"I'm working my tail off in school. But I would love to travel on a bicycle trip with you two.

Cooper shakes Eduard's hand and tells him, "OK, Eduard, I'm trusting you with a great looking package of a young lady. I may make a call to you just to check on my sister. Have a good trip, and thanks for your thoughts."

"One thing more, Coop." Eduard looks Cooper right in his eyes. "You have my promise, nothing will happen to her. She will have an unseen brother watching out for her. This I promise you. Nothing bad will happen. I had a cousin that went off to college and got into the wrong environment and fell apart. I know the stresses that come with college."

"If you give me your email address, Coop, I'll keep you posted. I'm not going to be a spy but I'll take an interest in her, this I promise you. Write in my notebook, your address, please. You'll get mine on my first letter. Both of us have to get going. Good luck on your bike ride, Coop. See you."

Coop walks back to where Sally waits, sitting on the wooden bench. "So you gave Eduard the rules? How many rules did you lay on him?"

"No, 'Miss Know It All.' "It's only that you have a very interesting young lad that will see you almost every day swimming and doing swimming exercises. Count this as the start of a new life and it will be very different from the one you're passing by. Ready lady, we are going bicycling touring."

Coop holds the bike so Sally can get on. "OK, Leader, where's our next campsite?"

"First through the Marines Camp Pendleton Base, if the they don't capture you with that new bicycling outfit you have on."

"What's wrong with what I'm wearing now?" "Nothing, except if I were to paint over your bicycling outfit you would look like a nude statue."

"Come on, it's not like that. Dr. Terri was with me when she bought this outfit for me.

"Well you can't see it, so why should you worry. Let's get moving sister or else we'll be biking in the dark and for bicycle tourers that's a no no."

Cooper and Sally picked up more than just some horn toots and few whistles going through the marine base.

"Coop, this is a place where Marines train?" "It's one of many. I've been told it's used prior to going overseas." "What is it, Coop, that men think women are impressed by men with whistles, horns or yells?" "Well, Sally, what you are saying is, that the male population should remain silent, with no yells or whistles, or showing their muscles, what would the female population do. Think about the whistles you received on this ride."

"Yes, I do. Not on one chance would I go out just with one of those whistlers or horn honkers.

"Say, Coop. What is that odor I smell? It's sure strong." "Yep, it sure is. You know that." "Certainly, Coop. That's why I asked. Now what is that smell?" "Oh that. That's mustard." "You mean like mustard in a bottle?"

"Well, fairly close. The real name is, let's see, hmmm. Got it. That's called Brassica from the Cruciferae family."

"How do you know that?" "That's one of the things I had to know to become an Eagle Scout. "What happened to the word mustard?"

"It's the same, interesting plant. It came to California by Father Sierra as he brought with him Black Mustard seeds from Europe and started scattering the seeds from Baja California clear up to San Francisco."

"Oh, I remember, Coop. He wanted to make a path that people could follow to the various Missions that became "The Road of Gold."

"Right, Sally. Also he gave farmers a weed pest. We might say he was our first polluter. From Father Sierra Black mustard has become one bad weed found from California to Mexico and most of our Western states.

"And this plant became one of the many plants called "Wind Tumblers". When these plants, like many, dry up by the late summer they become one of the Wind Tumbler plants.

"Yea, Coop, now I remember, we read the book "Road of Gold." I first thought is was finding gold in California. Yeah, Father Sierra became our first visiting polluter."

Then, it was along side old Highway 101, past a long narrow campground with plenty of rest stops and toilets.

Sally asks Cooper, "Are we passing through a camping area? I can smell bacon?"

"Yep. We are now passing a long narrow campground between the highway and the ocean. We'll follow the ocean for some time then camp at Doheny State Park. "Tomorrow we bicycle through the Los Angeles area and head toward La Canada. Hopefully we'll find a motel.

Then the next night we'll be camping or motel it in the start of the desert. We'll be on the edge of the El Paso and the San Gabriel Mountain areas."

"I thought we were going to bicycle in the desert?" "We are Sally. Deserts are not flat. Some hills wait for us. Tomorrow we bicycle to La Canada. There we'll meet one steep road. It's a killer." "Why go that way, Coop?" "It's the only way to get on the back side of the San Gabriel Mountains and to the desert. Cars and trucks have another route with four lanes or more. We are not allowed to bike on those roads.

"Why can't we bicycle on those wide roads, Coop?" "Because "know it all" politicians and highway engineers don't bicycle. They just don't understand bicycles or the people that bicycle. I guess they like the confines of cars. "You mean they, who ever they are, won't let bicyclers bicycle on certain roads?" "Exactly. If our politicians would learn to bicycle, well, that's a big maybe, our state would have more bicyclers out on the roads. We would have wide bicycle lanes and intelligent drivers."

"Sounds like it's a 'too easy' exercise for our elected officials to understand, Coop."

"I think you're right. Easy answers don't figure into politics or engineers thoughts. Where's the challenge?"

"Sally, soon we will enter the Los Angeles traffic on our way to—"

"Another campground?" "No. This time, I hope it will be a motel. If we push along without too many stops, we should be there before dusk." "You mean before dark? "I sure hope between dusk and dark. I don't like biking too late in the afternoon. Push on your pedals, lady, we've got miles to go." "We are going to stop for lunch, aren't we?" "Of course. This will be a long busy day for us, so keep stroking."

Cooper and Sally moved off the Coast Highway where they tackled horrendous traffic, noises and the smells of vehicle exhausts, and it was a nail biter trip for both of them.

They took lunch in a diner and Sally enjoyed the milkshake and a double hamburger. "I think Coop, I want all my lunches with hamburgers and milkshakes."

"Sounds great, sister, except tomorrow and the days to follow we may have to pack one or two sandwiches as we'll be in the high desert on Highway 395. Sometimes cafes show up and then they disappear.

Don't worry we'll make out just fine. Besides if you gain one pound more, you'll split your bicycle clothes."

"Here we go again. It's my clothes that you worry about?" "Not all the time, dear sister." "Coop, how about staying in motels instead of campouts, leader?" "Sorry, lady. It will be camp outs otherwise we'll run out of money and you said you like the night air, an outdoor fire, and the smell of wood burning."

"It must have been that swimmer, Eduard. By the way can you describe him to me? Just wondering, that's all."

"Finally it comes out. You are interested in this tall blond boy with big blue eyes. His hair has that swimmer's blond color. I suspect he doesn't wear a swimming cap unless he's in a meet."

"How tall, Coop, your height?" "About the same. Except he must weigh over 220 pounds, I'm at 190. I'll tell you this, he's a very good looking fellow." "Did Eduard show table manners when he was eating with us, last night?" "Excellent. He used the European method." "What's that?"

"He may be left handed but he didn't trade fork and knife while cutting a vegetable or a tough piece of meat one of the boys had brought. Eduard's manners, mind you, his camping table manners, were excellent. Even Dad or Mom would accept his manners. Now, why do you ask?

"Did he talk with his mouth full of food? You know, I like good manners and that last night I didn't hear his deep voice that sounded as if he a mouth full of food when he was talking.

"I could not hear food being consumed from Eduard. Oh, one boy, I guess toward the end of the table sure talked a lot with his mouth full of food. I hate that."

"Don't worry about his table manners. Last night they were perfect. I have a feeling sister you'll meet Eduard sooner than you thought when you report to college; as you are expected to be there two weeks before classes start.

"I'll bet he'll be at your side when you set one foot on the campus." "Remember this clue, Sally. Be sure to wear one of your bicycling outfits, I haven't seen the third one but if it's cut on the same lines as yesterday and today's outfits. On your first day on campus wear one of your bicycling clothes. That should grab more than one boy's attention."

"Coop. you're showing your evil mind. How many miles do we have to go?"

"About 45 more miles to La Canada. We'll grab a motel some where around there. Biking in this traffic gets one tired especially when the stroker, that's you sister, isn't pushing hard enough."

"I am, I am. I think the front engine is out of shape. It must be tough to exercise when on a date."

"Sally, I don't think you know what you said." "Dirty mind again, Coop." We pass the Rose Bowl and then comes one steep hill. "Push Sally, we're not at the top. What the heck is a station wagon doing that just passed us. Damn it. Now the driver is waving us over. It's some dumb woman who wants us to stop and we are not at the top. "I'm stopping Sally."

"Where in the world are you two going?" comes an articulated voice. Sally assumes it's the driver of the station wagon.

She knows her brother is upset.

Cooper replies, as he drags his feet to stop the tandem. "My sister and I are looking for a motel for the night. Could you direct us to a motel? Sally assumes it's the station wagon driver, then she hears, "We don't have any motels in this town. Come home with me." Cooper looks at the steep hill left to climb, and asks the lady, "Where do you live?"

She points on the road she stopped on. "Follow me. Our house is just a half block ahead. My name is Janice Smith. Let's get going; I have dinner on the stove. My husband is waiting for me."

Cooper and Sally bicycle behind Janice's station wagon. "What does she look like, Coop?"

"I'd say about in her earlier fifties. She's turning into her driveway and garage. Be ready to get off." Janice Smith waits for Cooper and Sally to dismount. "You can put your tandem in our garage, over there by the bench. Grab your clothes and what ever else and come in the back door."

Sally holds onto Cooper's arm and with her other arm she carries one of her panniers. They enter Janice's house from the back door.

Janice waits for them. "Come on in and meet my husband, William. Only our friends come into our house by the backdoor. You two are friends." Once in the kitchen, Cooper introduces his sister. "This is Sally Portage and I'm her brother, Cooper. My, Sally, you have a great looking bicycle outfit on. It's your colors all the way."

"Thank you, Mrs. Smith. My brother thinks it is rather bold." "Bold? Poof. You've have the figure and with your blond hair you look great. OK, now where are you two going?"

"Yosemite." Replies Cooper. "I promised my sister I would take her to Yosemite after she graduates. So Sally has held me to my promise." "What a great brother you have. "Sally dear, do you have a visual problem?" Inquires Mrs. Smith.

"Yes, I have. I'm slowly going blind. It started when I was about six years old."

"William and I are teachers and we have one boy in our school that is blind. The way he gets around school one may not realize he is visually impaired. I have him in my class now. He's a good lad."

A trim fifty or so man enters the kitchen from the back door. "William, I want you to meet a couple of bicyclers." William Smith enters the kitchen, and there introductions all around.

"That's a mighty fine looking bicycling outfit you have on young lady. Janice, you should get a bicycling outfit like Sally has."

"At my age? Don't be silly." "Certainly. Last summer Janice and I bicycled across the United States from New York to here. What was the name of the girl biking on a tandem with her husband and she was blind? Man, could those two move that bicycle.

"I kept looking to see where the motor was kept. She could really pump that bicycle. Yep. The motor was on the rear of the bicycle."

"And all this time, Bill, I thought you were checking out her figure." "Well, I just kept wondering how you would look in an outfit like hers. We arrived home with two days left on our vacation. We had a grand time and met some wonderful bicyclers along our way. So you two are going to Yosemite over Tioga Pass?"

"Yes Sir, Mr. Williams, we are." "Forget the Mister part, Cooper, use Jack. Have you done this trip before?" "Yes Sir, Mr. oops, Jack, I have done the ride three times entering the park from the west. I had no problems except the traffic and that climb up to Mariposa."

"I know what you mean, Coop. I did it once, years ago. Isn't that climb almost straight up?

"It sure was to me, Jack. Probably the steepest I've traveled on." "I don't think you two will have any problems once reach the top of the hill, either. The way your sister is dressed, she surely is an eye catcher.

"Better show you to your room. Are twin beds, OK?" "We do when we are camping, Jack." "Great. I'll show you two where your bathroom is. Take a shower and I'll have towels out. We'll have dinner and tell each other bicycling stories."

During dinner the stories regarding bicycling and touring brought many laughs.

Cooper relates, "My sister was wearing the most outlandish bicycling outfit. We met three boys bicycling to San Diego and they were bug-eyed seeing my sister in a, well, it sure was, very form fitted bicycle clothes.

"Even cars were slowing down when passing us on the highway and there was lots of horn honking from cars and trucks when they passed by us."

"Well, Cooper, if I were diving by maybe I would have honked." Remarks Jack.

Janice adds, "Even at your age you would have honked your horn passing these two bicyclers especially if you had a horn on your bicycle."

"I don't think so, Janice. Maybe a whistle would be more catching." Sally stands up and tells the three, "Well I figure out how I would handle my situation, I'm going to bed. I've had a big day. See you all tomorrow morning. It was a lovely dinner, Mrs. Smith. Goodnight all."

Cooper hops up and helps Sally down the hallway to their bedroom. Coop returns back to the dining room. "Well, one to bed and another one is ready for bed. "This week will be a learning experience for both of us. So far, it's going along great. I want to thank you all for your hospitality.

Cooper continues. "I can add this: Though my sister is just about blind she can recognize people by the way they talk, by the way they eat, how they smell, and their manners, she judges them constantly.

"With the three boys, we met at a campground, she pinned one boy by the way he talked with a mouth full of food. Another boy that kept squirming in his seat as he sat on one side of her. And the the third boy, she was surprised by his good overall manners. Sally was somewhat taken back.

"This, I think, is the first time I have any knowledge of my sister's interest by any boy and that lad had gentlemanly manners."

Janice leans over to Cooper, "You know I have spent years in classrooms and a few times I have had nearly blind children. I think we forget that their senses don't expand with the loss of one sense, like Sally.

"They seem to be able to hone their other senses to a fine degree, and your sister has sharp senses working for her.

May I suggest giving her a little more slack in your rope you have on her. This is good time to free her a bit; don't you agree, Jack?"

"Absolutely. Your sister is miles ahead of girls like her even without similar problems in vision. My word, I have a classroom full of girls that couldn't hold a candle to Sally and her grown up approach to life, especially her life and these kids can see. "Your family and you have done a great job of working with Sally. What your family have done should be in a book of "How Two" I'm certain about that."

"You know Jack", Cooper mentions, "I've really been thinking about what you two have said.

"This is one reason we are on this bicycle ride. I'm trying to give Sally more room for her independence. It's tough move for me. Maybe it's like letting a trophy fish off your line to swim another day.

"Tomorrow, I have plans to let Sally pay our bills, make the arrangements where we'll stay the night and just be in charge of the clues I will give her.

"With your advice and my help we'll have Sally ready for college and independence even more than she is now, if that is possible."

"Before you go to bed, Coop, I have one more question. Does Sally know anything about self protection, like Judo, or one of the self protection moves like for her defense?"

"She sure does, Jack. She's had classes since she was in the third grade with this warning: Do not play around using this defense. Use it only in time of trouble."

"Is she any good in self defense being blind?" "Darn good. If she can feel a person's hand she knows immediately if it's the right or left hand. If someone were to grab her from behind, her moves are almost automatic.

"With just a pat on her rear end, or her breast, if she does not know the person, Sally becomes a tiger.

"In grade school many a boy found out this was bad news for him. In high school a boy tried to run his hand over her breasts and he'll never do that again.

"I was told she had that boy on his back with both of his legs spread apart ready to stomp on him before a teacher pulled her away.

"Her self-defense from then on was well respected. Besides her swimming she keeps up on her defense. In a swimming pool if she thinks someone is getting friendly the wrong way her training comes out. She's a tiger."

Jack Smith replies, "You know, Cooper, just looking at her one wouldn't guess that Sally has that ability."

"I agree, Jack, her legs and arm muscles feel like steel cords. She's in shape the year around. One would never guess this young lady is a First Class tiger when threatened.

"Cooper, see you two in the morning, I'm up at six in the morning every morning. Would hot cakes and pure maple syrup fit you two for breakfast? Janice needs one day to catch up on her sleep?"

"Same as Mom. She always wants to start the week off being caught up on her sleep. OK, see you just after six.

"Home cooked breakfast is hundred times better than a restaurant with cool hot cakes and cold syrup."

"You're on, Cooper. I'll be sure everything will be hot. See you two in the morning."

# CHAPTER 11

COOPER AND SALLY, IN the morning after a huge breakfast, leave La Canada and the Smiths with promises to keeping them updated on their bicycle ride. This was one very steep climb that nearly lasted hours of sweat, and burning muscles as they tackled Highway 2. This was one grind always up and up.

"Yea Gods, Coop, are we near the top?" "Not yet Sally. Want to stop and rest?" "No. It's too hard to start up. Let's keep going." "Further ahead, Sally, we'll stop at a rest area and split a sandwich that Fred made for us." "OK, Buster, I'm going to hold you on that promise." Two hours later they reach to top. Before them are three picnic benches, tables and an outdoor toilet.

"Fair enough, lady. We'll stop here and take a break. We have a table and benches. Ready?"

"I believe I was ready an hour ago, Coop. Hold the bike for me, I'm getting off now. My rear end is numb. That was some mountain we climbed up. Park the bike and lead me to a soft bench I want to stretch out, now."

"I'll take you over to a picnic bench. No padding, but it's a bench." "Well, that's better than a bicycle seat. Where's that sandwich?"

"I'm getting it. We will have a few more miles of mostly down hill. Wait there, I'm going to get my camera and take a few pictures of one pooped girl.

"Our bicycle ride the rest of the afternoon should be down hill, about 20 some miles to Lancaster and another 25 plus miles, then we'll stop in Mojave for the night.

"Is it a motel you want, Sally or a camp someplace in the desert, tonight?"

"I think the sun is getting to my guide. Of course a motel might be my last motel before Yosemite."

Coop walks over to his bicycle and takes, from his handle bar bag, two cameras. One is his favorite that he bought with his own money. It was slightly over one thousand dollars and the other one went for one hundred eighty dollars.

Cooper walks around Sally to get various pictures with his expensive camera then he takes a number of shots of Sally with his small light camera.

Cooper places the cameras on another picnic table that's closer to the bicycles.

He returns to his sister. "Would you like a quick snack before Lancaster or Palm Dale?" "Either one. You bet. I have to wash out my bicycle clothes before they begin to smell." Cooper, during this stop, tells Sally, "We are about to enter the Mojave Desert. Temperatures should be higher and we'll have a head wind until we turn off to Tioga Pass."

"You mean we'll be climbing and always into a headwind. I want to resign my bicycle ride with one cruel brother."

"Wait a minute, Sally. It's gradual climb. Some areas along Highway 395 do have some hills but not anything like we just came up. In fact, you'll hardly notice it. It's . . . .

Before he can finish his description, an older car with a man driving stops close to their bicycles and cameras.

This car is about 15 years old. Cooper watches the car and the driver. Something is not right flashes through Cooper's mind.

The people, in this car, just sit in the car and appear to look at Cooper and Sally along with the bicycles and the two cameras on the far table next to the red tandem bicycle.

These items, the bicycle and cameras are closer to the old car than Sally and Cooper.

Sally starts to say something and Cooper, with a low voice he says, "Hold it, Sally, and just be quiet for a minute."

"What's up, Coop?" In a low voice he tells his sister, "Just be quiet and let me handle this. We have some guests, I'm not happy to see right now." He watches the two people remaining in the car, and appear to be talking. Now the man exits the car and walks up to the picnic bench holding the cameras.

He says to the lady, still in the car, "Don't they have good looking cameras?"

"Yes, they do." came the voice inside the car. "Wouldn't you like to have a camera or both like these?" "It would be nice, but leave those people alone." "I don't know about that. I've always wanted a camera and there's two here." Cooper is sizing up his problem. The two cameras are where the stranger is standing. The tandem is by one table beyond the cameras.

In his handle bar bag is a German baton whip. The baton when stretched out becomes one stinging whip.

Cooper was given this whip from an uncle that was in the American Army in Germany doing some training some years ago.

Uncle Ben said to Cooper, "This baton makes into a heck of a deadly whip when you snap it out. It stings like hell. Maybe you can use this in case of a bicycling problem, sometime.

"You sure won't be carrying a pistol, as that is a no no, as a pistol can be a dangerous concealed weapon. This baton isn't."

Cooper is analyzing how many steps he must take to reach his handle bar bag. He's thinking: If I don't go to the cameras but to my bicycle that may not be a threatening move. I'll get Sally in on this.

Coop said out loud, "Sally, I'll get your lipstick for you. I thought you put it in my handle bar bag."

Sally is thinking: It's in my handle bar bag, not his. He knows that. There has to be a reason he said that. "Thanks, Coop. I could use it."

Coop slowly walks to his handle bar bag and opens it. He places one hand into the bag and grabs the German whip still concealed in the bag. He's thinking, it's no use showing it now. I'll wait if he makes the wrong move then I'll bring it out. I'll just move my hand around like I'm looking for Sally's lipstick."

It's quiet at this picnic place. No cars have come by. The man is still looking at the cameras and Cooper appears to be looking for Sally's lipstick.

Finally the woman in the car hollers out to the driver, "Just forget it, Ralph. We have to get going. We are not even close to Nevada. Leave them two alone, Ralph, climb in and let's go."

"Well, I sure would like one or two of those cameras." "Not here. Let's go." Ralph walks back to his car. Before getting in his car, he takes one more look at the cameras. "I sure would like, at least, one camera." "I just told you: Leave those two alone. We've been here too long.

Lets go." With a slam of the car door off went the old car and a sigh of relief came from Cooper. Cooper has memorized the car's license plate number and color, age, and make of the car. He quickly writes in his the diary the important information and thinks:

When we reach Lancaster, in less than an hour, I'll talk to the police and tell them what happened and what I heard, and where the two people may be going.

"Ready to go, partner?"

"You bet I'm ready. I'm hungry. What were those two people up to?" "I don't know, but they are gone. Let's go." "Why did you mention my lipstick? You knew where I keep it and it's never in your handle bar bags unless you're doing something I didn't know about?"

"Well I just didn't trust those people and I had to get to my bicycle without alerting them. I think you handled your part very well.

"Let's get this show going and lunch is just a little over an hour from here and almost all down hill."

"I think I'm going to like this part of our trip. Lead the way, boss." Exactly one hour later, the tandem bicycle unloads two happy bicyclers that had a beautiful downhill bicycle ride for most of the 20 miles.

Sally mentions to Cooper, "I think two hamburgers with everything on it will hold me over till we reach the motel at Mojave. "Please make that with a large vanilla milkshake. After all it's only 32 miles left today the way our bicycles travel."

"Close, Sally." Lets grab a booth. I'll show you, then I have to make a phone call."

"Don't tell me it's another girl you have on your dating string that lives around here?"

"Somehow I believe I missed this town while collecting dates. Stay seated and I'll be right back."

"Could you show me to the restroom before asking some desert girls for a date?"

'Sure, take my arm and let's go." "Pardon me, sir, I'll take your daughter to the rest room for you." A young waitress offered her services.

Sally responds, "Yep, he did it. Now he knows someone in Lancaster. Let me take your elbow, Miss, and you can be my guide. My brother needs a telephone."

"This is your brother? Hmmm, I'll still take you. The telephone is next to the cashier in the corner. Here's my arm and follow me. What is your name?"

Off went the girls and Cooper headed for the telephone. He made his call and he was told a police officer will be right there to take down the his observations that Cooper gave to them over the telephone.

This was quick. Sally has not returned when a police officer arrives at the restaurant and catches Cooper's eyes. He slides into the seat opposite Cooper.

The first thing after introductions is: "I'm Officer Rickman. I think we have a hit. One more time, tell me what they looked like, their car description, the license plate numbers and letters. You mentioned you thought they were headed to Nevada?"

Cooper begins when Sally returns with the young waitress. The police officer immediately stands and offers his seat to Sally.

Cooper mentions, "No, Sally can sit next to me. Officer Rickman needs some information from us regarding the people we met at that picnic area after we left La Canada."

The waitress pulls out a card and hands it to Cooper. "Any time in your travels please stop and give me the latest news on Sally. She's such a lovely girl and very independent. I'd like to keep track of her.

"Maybe our mighty Officer Rickman will order, if he's not too busy." She gives the officer a poke on his shoulder.

Cooper looks at her card, her name is Franziska Zimmerman and then looks at her blond hair, deep blue eyes, clear skin with only a dab of makeup on.

Cooper answers, "I hope you will stay current with Sally. My sister will be a freshman in USC this fall. May I include myself in that opportunity?"

"It will be my pleasure as I'm on my senior trip at USC. "Now I'm your waitress, are you ready to order? I really want to keep track of Sally." During lunch, the policeman stayed writing everything Cooper and Sally could remember.

Also, he was able to find out, from Sally's hearing the two, in the car, the lady had a nasal twang and a distinct New England voice.

"We'll get those two. If it's the right couple we have enough to keep those two behind bars for twenty years.

"I'll tell you two this, our Nevada borders will be checked within one hour. They can't get to a Nevada border any quicker.

"If they try to turn around, we'll get them. Thank you two for the alertness. Any police officer would love to have witnesses be as complete with information as you two have done. So, you're headed to Yosemite?"

"When we catch those two, I'll have the Highway Patrol stop you and give you the results before you reach Tioga Pass.

"Bike carefully and we'll give you the good news in a couple of days. Thank you both again. Cooper, will you be passing this way soon?"

"Not that I know of Officer, why?" The officer leans close to Cooper. "Well Franziska will be a senior at USC this fall and she laid on you a possible date. "How do I know? I have three female teenagers at home and I can tell a possible date in the dark even when there's no conversations.

My wife and I live right across the street from Franziska. I've known her before she was riding her tricycle.

"I'll keep nods to Franziska Zimmerman on our catching those people." Officer Rickman stands up and with, "Good Luck to the both of you." He leaves with a wave of his hand and a touch on Franziska's shoulder.

"Well, brother, I'm impressed by the way you collect girls. Now I'll have a female watching me, in school that is, to find out how my brother is getting along. What's it worth to you if I don't always tell her the truth?"

"Nice girls don't do that to their brothers. Now try to be nice." After lunch it's a little over 32 miles to the town of Mojave. They have gone over 20 miles by now.

Sally, pumping in the rear seat, asks, "I always thought the desert is hot but never considered it would be this hot and so windy. It's like bicycling in a pizza furnace. What about you, leader?"

"Well let's see . . ." "Don't get so scientific in your analysis, Coop. Just tell me how hot is it?"

"I'm trying to tell you. According to the temperature gauge on my handle bar it's only 99 degrees and that could be the heat bouncing up from the black highway. Don't worry it hasn't hit a 100 yet."

"OK, how far is that town we'll stay in, ugh, Mojave? It's not a quiet town?"

"Nope. A lot of trucks stop there for the night. We'll try to find a motel slightly off the beaten path, if possible. In two hours we'll see Mojave."

"We'll see it? Huh? Any pools or sauna's there?" "If the wind, sand and dust hasn't made the motel owners drain their saunas or pools, we'll take advantage of the facilities. Sometimes the wind gets so strong and the dust is so thick, they have to drain pools and saunas. We'll see when we get there."

After about one-hour and a half of bicycling on a fairly straight and level, but busy road, Sally and Cooper arrive in Mojave.

Sally announces, "There are sure a lot of truck noises around us, Coop." "You're right. We are on highway 14 and getting close to Highway 395 that goes up the backside of the Sierra. "Remember our ride up to Dr. McGill's ranch? The mountains on our right were the Sierra but over the years it became Sierras now. Once a single name. "When we turned left off Highway 5, the Sierra mountains then became the Cascades.

"The Sierra, a Spanish name, means, one long mountain range. "Sally, hold the bicycle. I'll ask in this service station about motels that are quiet."

In a minute Cooper returns. "They have one about two blocks off from the highway 395." It's only four in the afternoon and we may find a vacancy. Lets go."

At the Silver Eagle Motel, Cooper checks in with two beds and they have a large enough room for the tandem.

The motel owner suggests, "We serve dinner and an early breakfast." The owner continues, "The motel pool and sauna are empty. All last week a lot of sand and dust blew in. All pools and saunas on highway 395 are also empty, but we have a shower in the tub. You can now soak those muscles. We have lots of hot water."

Cooper tells Sally, "Take advantage of the bath as we'll soon be camping in the desert with no luxuries."

"Easy for you to say, sport." While walking the bicycle to their room, Sally asks; "Where do we go to the bathroom when we are out in the bare desert? Are you going to hold up a blanket or tent for me?"

Cooper is smiling at his sister's innocence. She's camped before, except only in county, state or federal parks. This will be a new experience for her.

He tells her, "I'll find a place in the desert that is away from the highway. Let me warn you now, squat where I tell you, otherwise you might meet a cactus plant that has very sharp spines or needles. Some of them can pierce right through a person. Indians used cactus spines for killing small animals for food."

"Where will you be during this episode of my life, Coop?" "Probably holding a screen so you can't be seen from the road. With one hand I will hold the tarp and with the other hand, my nose." "Darn it, be serious, Coop. This is all new to me. I need your help." "Don't worry about it, Sally. There are depressions in the desert where one can't be seen. We'll look for those if we camp away from rest areas or cemeteries."

"Cemeteries? You are telling me we might camp in cemeteries. Is that correct!"

"Forget it. We'll motel it." "Have you camped in cemeteries while bicycling?" "Many times. I go to the back of the cemetery, if its not raining and find a place where I can't be seen from the highway.

"If it's raining, then I'll put up my solo tent. It's hard to see in the dark. Even the people in the cemetery don't seen to care. Anyway they never complained to me. I don't leave a mess and try to leave before sunrise."

"Count me out camping in any cemetery with you or without you. I would be awake all night, worrying." "Worrying about what, Sally?" "Ghosts, you dummy. Who's taking the first shower before we have dinner?" "I'll show you the shower, Sally. I'll lay out the towels you can use.

Your panniers are on the foot of the bed. "Take the one with the change of clothes you have. After my shower we'll have dinner. The restaurant is close to us. That's where we will have breakfast tomorrow morning.

"On your feet lady and grab what you need. We are in the desert and its warm outside. So don't over dress. Wait. Don't under dress especially, please."

After leading Sally to the bathroom and letting her familiarize herself, he turns on the shower and leaves.

Cooper sits on his bed and dials out to Lancaster and to the restaurant they had lunch the other day.

He can hear the phone ringing, then a 'Good Evening, Lancaster's German restaurant, May I help you?" He pauses before answering. That voice must be Franziska's. "Do you deliver?"

"Certainly, what you like to order, Sir." "How about sending a delightful German lass with ski blue eyes and a natural blond waitress to deliver three dinners to Mojave tonight. It that is problem? We have reservations for three dinners here in the restaurant. Well, to be honest, our dinner reservations includes you."

"Uh, hmm, this must be uh, Cooper. You are slightly out of our territory. How's the bicycle ride coming along?

"Great. No problems. I just had to call and thank you for all your help with my sister when we were in your café."

"You called me just to say that?" "No. I would like to get ahead of the rest of the boys and ask you out for dinner tonight, then after our classes start this fall, another dinner. I know it is a brash move on my part, please excuse that. I'll drive to USC to see my sister but I would like to know you better tonight during dinner. Am I too impulsive?"

"Let's see, tonight. You two are about 25 miles or so from Lancaster. What motel are you in?"

"Silver Spur Inn." "Is that the one that's on the right and back off the highway?" "Exactly." "Great. I'm off tonight. I'll take a quick shower and be cleaned up and I'll see you two in 45 minutes. What room do you have?" "I think it is, let's see, ah, the key, it's Room 18 down stairs.

I'll leave a light on for you." "Wrong motel, Cooper. See you two in 45 minutes. Cooper you have to be quick with your shower. I'm not walking into your room if you are not up and dressed. Bye."

Sally had come out from the shower and had heard one side of the phone conversation. "Could that be Franziska from Lancaster?"

"OK, big ears, you're right. We are having a guest for dinner, so what?" "I knew it. Franziska wanted to know all about you when she guided me to the restaurant's toilet area. Of course I didn't tell her everything. "She told me she would like to know you better. She's a senior at USC.

She thought she would invite you to a dinner and dance at her school. I gave her your address and phone number at Poly. "So you jumped the gun and she's coming here. Good for you, The Lover Boy of San Diego. Now you have a girl from Lancaster." "You say anything about my past and you, young lady, you may not see the sun rise in the morning." "Yeah. Take your shower, maybe a cold shower, and shave or I will tell her your past and might just embellish it somewhat if that is possible. Get a move on, Romeo."

True to her word, Franziska knocks on door 18. Out steps Cooper, dressed in white hiking shorts and a white T-shirt and carrying his white white tennis shoes. He is still wiping his face with a motel towel. He glares at Sally. "For two cents I'll leave my baby sister here alone in this room while we will have a nice quiet dinner, Franziska."

"No no, Cooper," Franziska answers, "That's not fair. Sally was just alerting me. After all, we girls must stick together. Right Sally?"

"Right. Well, brother, are you taking two ladies to dinner or do we ladies have go to the highway and flag a trucker for company and dinner?"

"It's not an easy choice you gave me, Sally. Let's see, dinner alone or dinner with two smart conniving ladies. Well life, at times, is chancy and I'll take a chance tonight. Let me get my shoes on and we will have dinner if my upstart sister stays quiet during dinner and that's a near impossibility thought."

Franziska stands up. "Here's my left elbow, Sally. If your brother can find his right elbow we'll all go for dinner, together, and we'll leave the truckers alone, this time."

Dinner was time to become acquainted with laughs from all three. Franziska tells the group she is one of three children, the other two are in the Navy. Franziska is attending USC, as a senior, and majoring in history and hopes to continue into a Masters program.

Sally pipes up that she will be a freshman in USC this fall. Then adds, maybe I'll have a boy friend when I enter college."

"What. My word, Sally, you already have a boy friend in college?" "Well, not exactly. We met at a campground and he was nice and said he will watch for me; he is a sophomore and on the swimming team. I hope to be on the swimming team. Right, Coop?" "My head is spinning." Franziska enters the conversation. "My word, you two are fast workers. I didn't even start to date until nearly the end of my junior year in college and that wasn't all that exciting. I don't drink or smoke and lots of the guys do.

"Then the book worms are only interested in books. Well, we'll see how my Master's program works out. What about you, Cooper?"

He has had his head on his chin just listening to the girls talk. "I have just school friends. Not a serious one in the litter. Yes, I know lots of girls at my college but in the last year of my architectural course, it requires one heck of a lot of study and reading and 24 hours in my lab work.

"Usually it's a group out for Saturday night and none of them really dance. I'm the only one who dances. We drink a little beer and argue over our lessons and lab problems and the classes they assign us to. Everyone of us is in a different program. We share knowledge listen to our progress or losses, but that's all. I have a kind of sainted life right now."

Franziska replies, "Well it didn't take you long to ask me out for a date. What frat house is yours on campus?"

I have an apartment the size of a broom closet, that's all. I can't go the frat route and never could. I'm getting close to my degree. Engineering is next.

"My hours are hellish and a lot of time is spent alone in the lab. When I saw you with Sally I just wished we could meet sometime. I must give Sally credit for that and only that. Let's order."

Dinner lasted until they closed the café at eleven. Sally received a hug and kiss from Franziska. Cooper waited and finally closed his eyes and puckered up his lips and waited. He received a very quick kiss and this remark, "I'm calling for a date this fall, Coop and you had better honor it."

Coop reached over grabbed her hands and holding them he answered Franziska, "Only after inviting you to our home for Thanksgiving. Is that a deal?"

"My head is spinning Coop, but I'll say yes now." "May we seal the invitation with a real kiss." Sally waits a short time then replies, "Coop. We have miles to go so just shake hands and let's go." Franziska reaches over to Sally saying, "Love you Sally. Take care of your brother. We both need him. In a few months we'll meet again. I'm in love with you both."

Sally holds on to Copper's hand as Cooper watches Franziska leave the restaurant. "Well, lover boy," Sally remarks, "That was some quick romance or was it a passing fancy?"

"Dear sister, she's a keeper. Let's hit the sack as we have miles to go before we reach Yosemite."

While having breakfast the next morning, Cooper asked the waitress, "Is there a café, for lunch, between Mojave and Olancha?"

She stops and thinks. "I believe there's one called Buzzard Cafe. Well once, when it was open, it was called that."

An almost straight bike ride at near eleven o'clock in the morning Cooper sees 'Buzzard Café' showing up on the left side of 395 Highway.

A Black and White Highway Patrol car is parked in front along with two long haul trucks.

In the café went Cooper with Sally holding on to Cooper's right elbow. Sally is wearing her pink bicycling outfit. All conversation stops when this bicycle team enters the café.

Two truckers and the Highway Patrol Officer were having lunch. In one corner a man was peeling apples.

Off to the left of the small café is the kitchen and a grey haired lady appeared to be the cook and the man with the apples could be her husband from the conversations that ran around the room.

"Holy cow, what a bicycle outfit just walked in the Buzzard Café. Where are you two headed besides to some wild gathering? This question came from the Highway Patrol Officer.

Cooper replies, "We're on our way to Yosemite." "Are you bicycling with that red bicycle that's outside?" "We sure are." "Hmmm." Then the officer looks at the two truckers. "Stick your eyes back into head and listen to me. Tell you what we'll do." Mac and you, Red, when you get on the road send a call out to your trucker bunch to be on the look our for a, you are her brother?"

"Yes I am." Replied Cooper. "Are you the two that clued the officers in Lancaster, yesterday regarding two people at a rest area?" "That's us."

"Lancaster officers called me this morning. They wanted to make sure you are notified. They have an arm length of charges against those two in California and three other states.

"They told me, tell them, a brother with his sister with a 'woower' bicycling outfit are bicycling to Yosemite. "If you see them, and they won't be hard to miss, as the lady with a bicycle outfit, you've never seen before. If they are in a problem, stop and give them a hand.

"They sure can't miss them the way the young lady is dressed. Man o man, what a flashy outfit she has on. Miss, are you blind?"

"Yes I am." Replies Sally.

The Highway Patrol Officer continues, "I'll tell you what, Mac, let your truck bunch know what outfit she has on. Wow.

"I've been twenty years on this highway and I've never seen a bicycler with such a colorful outfit on. Can you do that as I'll alert our officers the same news."

Cooper is astounded by that request. "Golly, fellows, I've done some biking but never ran across your offer, all three of you."

One of the truckers answered Cooper, "First it's not you, it's your sister. No. It's not just us but the whole bunch of us. There is a far distance between towns and help when traveling this route. We let our gang be on alert when we see people like you two doing what you're doing. And if the bicycler or car has a problem, we stop.

"Besides we don't get much chance to talk to people on 395, so we watch out for bicyclers and broken down cars. Of course, that outfit your sister has should stop any car or truck even if you have no problem but just stopped to see some views.

"When we tell them other truck jocks your sister is mighty pretty and is wearing the most flashy biking outfit I've ever seen on this road, you'll get plenty of help if there's a need. I can hardly wait to tell all of them about the bicycling outfit."

From that moment on, conversations and questions ran the full gauntlet of bicycle stories these men have seen or heard about.

Cooper and Sally stayed in the café talking until an apple pie came out of the oven. With ice cream on top of the two slices of warm apple pie, Cooper and Sally finally finished their lunch. Now they leave and one hour and a half has passed from lunch and conversations.

Their evening stop should be at Olancha. It might be in the evening. Cooper tells Sally, "We will not bike in the dark no matter how many flashlights we tie on our bicycles. There is no bicycling after the sun goes down."

"How can I tell, Coop, when it's dark?" "Easy. That's when we stop bicycling. We may have to camp out in the High Desert. No problem, but lets pickup speed and try to get to Olancha before dusk." Along the way, when long haul trucks going south or north, pass the tandem bicycle, the drivers blink their lights and blow their air horns. The truckers always receive a wave from Sally.

These horn blasts gave Sally and Cooper knowledge that if they have a problem with their bicycle, help will be close by.

While crossing a railroad track, Cooper tells his sister, "Sally, we'll make Olancha before dark. In just a couple of more miles we'll see lights. Maybe we'll find a motel."

"And if my leader can't find a motel, what do we do next, boss?" "No problem. Maybe there is a cemetery around. I see our stop ahead." "Wait just one minute, Cooper. I'm not sleeping in a cemetery for any good or poor reason, brother."

"Well, then you can stay awake and talk to the ghosts." Into Olancha they bicycle. With the small amount of motels in Olancha, they are all filled up.

The owner of the restaurant tells Cooper where they might be able to camp.

"Well, you can go a short distance on Highway 190 to Dirty Sock Campground Camp or camp next to my work shop, by the garage, for the night. It might be a trifle noisy from some of the local regulars, and some are real live locals. Use our toilets. I'll keep a watch over you two if the beer drinkers get too loud."

"Thank you, but I don't believe we'll hear much noise; may we use your toilet facilities to change clothes before dinner?"

"Sure can. But I kinda wanted your sister to keep that pink bicycling outfit on."

Cooper laughs and says, "Wait till I tell my sister that." The next morning Coop and Sally enter the restaurant to have breakfast. The owner came up to them and asked, "Was it quiet enough for you two last night?"

"Didn't hear a thing until, I guess it was that rooster that woke us up in the morning."

"I'm sorry I forgot to tell you about that guy. He wakes everyone in Olancha when he lets going in the morning." Cooper explains, "No problem. We are headed for Independence but will stop at Manzanar National Historic Site along the way. May not be able to reach Independence, if not, we'll camp out."

"I know what you mean. I think I spent almost a day going through their exhibit. It's a good learning project for anyone who came after World War Two. Well, enjoy. Ah, I'm covering your breakfast, just handle the tip."

"But why?" "Your sister has another bicycle outfit on. I was told by the truck drivers and three Highway patrol men about the outfits your sister is wearing and they weren't kidding."

Sally is fussing around the counter wondering about getting some chips to add to the lunch. The lady, behind the long counter, keeps a running conversation with Sally telling her what it is that Sally asks about or points to.

A man, also appearing to be shopping, bumps into Sally three or four times. He has pasty colored skin, just as if he has stayed away from the sun for some time.

This portly built man continues to bump Sally, and she keeps excusing herself, each time. This stranger stays close to Sally and now hears where she and her brother are going on their long bicycle ride. He's thinking, her brother? Could it be? When he receives that bit of information, he quickly leaves the store.

With short quick steps he reaches a small old blue Volkswagen pickup. He hops in on the passenger side. The driver looks at his passenger. "Hmmm, You look happy. Did you get some trick, as you been gone a long time?"

"Better than that, Rick." "You going to share, Tony?" "You're not going to believe this. Remember two or three years or so when we were caught poaching on that ranch up north?"

"You mean them two guys that came at us. One was on horse back yelling his head off and charged us and that other guy was running.

"Yeah, I remember. And them two guys beat our asses when we could have had those two girls? Yeah, I still remember after hundred and eighty days in the cooler, so what?"

"I found one of those girls and the guy that was running." "You saw them two, right here in this desert?"

"Yep. Listen now. That blond gal can't see. She is blind as hell. Her brother and his sister are on bicycles going, I think, to Yosemite."

"She sure wasn't blind that day we saw those gals. You didn't talk to her?"

"No. What do you think I'm crazy?" "We'll snatch her, she's blind as a stone. We take her brother out and we got something we can play with to pay for our 180 days in that smelly thing called a prison. We can bury her in one of them salt beds. Him too."

"OK. How we going to do it. We just pick her up and drive away?" "No, you crazy. We follow them where they are going on 395. At a certain desolate spot we grab her. Shoot the brother and bury him. Just somewhere he can't be found. I would say we can pound her for a couple of days and nights. Perhaps some distance from that old cabin we saw when we were driving on that rocky road by Montezuma Peak in that real desolate place called uh, something like Esmeralda."

"Yeah, I remember that. What a desolate peace of nothing that place is. There's not a car or house anywhere."

"Right. We can even chase her around that forgotten piece of landscape for hours. She can't go anywhere. She's blind. We can call that fore play. Get her good and sweaty before we bang her."

"OK, how we going to get her?" "Well, we know they are going to Yosemite. That road between Big Pine and Independence we can find a place to get them. That's a straight stretch of road. That's where we grab her. "What about the guy or brother, what ever, How we handle him?"

"He's the first one we should take out. We got six pops in that old 45 rod that's under the driver's seat. Easy. We'll just keep our eye on them as we cruise 395. When they hit that straight stretch we do our job. Lets move out now and find a good spot for us to wait."

"You mean pretend we ran out of gas or we need a push like our battery ain't working too good."

"That's it. Good thinking."

Sally finally decides on what type of potato chips she wants. Reaching in her purse she selects the required amount of money. Sally speaks out, "Ready Coop."

Cooper slides along side his sister as she is paying the clerk. The clerk asks Cooper, "Does this young lady have a problem seeing?"

Cooper smiles and nudges Sally. "No problem. She's only blind." "But, but she counted out the change correctly." "Well, she should. My sister started losing her eyesight years ago. So she had a chance to practice constantly, as if she were blind, so when the time came she slipped into it, like a pro."

"Is that your bicycle, that long red bicycle, yours, outside?" "No. It's Sister Sally's tandem bicycle, the red one. "So you're the ones we were told, at least by five truck drivers and three highway officers. "Just be on the lookout for a brother and his blind sister, on a red tandem bicycle, bicycling to Yosemite. I can't believe it's you two."

She runs around her counter, to touch Sally on the arm, then gives her a big hug. "Wait till I tell my seventeen year old daughter what I saw today. Honey, I'll never complain about any problem or anything my daughter fishes up. Thank you for coming in and have a safe bike ride."

Sally was smiling along with Cooper. Then Sally asked, "The man ahead of me, I think he was about my size, "Does he live around here?"

"Yeah I think so. He lives somewhere in Nevada someplace. I never trusted that man and really I never knew him either. I think he got himself in trouble up north doing something, and went to jail for a couple of years. I don't even know his name. Why did you ask?"

Sally reaches for Cooper's hand. "He kept bumping into me when I was deciding on a bag of potato chips, that's all." "Honey, you should have told me. I would have thrown his dirty ass out of here in a second. Well he's gone. I saw him leave with another man with him in an old blue pickup. Is there a problem?"

"No, No. I just wondered." Sally puts her hand out and shakes the clerks hand. "Thank you for telling me about the chips. Well, Mr. Portage, lets go." Standing by their Tandem bicycle, Sally asks, "Where's our camp sight leader." "Well, we kicked a few hours messing around. We have about 30 miles to Lone Pine. It'll take about three hours. "We may arrive late, lets make it a motel tonight. By the time we arrive it well be getting dark. Maybe tomorrow night we'll camp out. "Before we leave, what was that all about you and a man when you were in that store talking to the lady that runs that department?". "What story, Coop?" "Holy Smokes, Sally. That story about a man in the store.

Remember?" "Well you remember our first year up at Terri's ranch and the two men Maggie and I found pouching? That was when you and Meredith came at us like a two rabid screaming animals."

Yeah I remember, but where does that guy fit in?" "I think one of those men was behind me in that store. I kinda recognized his voice. He kept bumping me. Of course I couldn't see him. His voice and a smell I caught, well he reminded me of that day with Maggie and you and Meredith. That's all, Coop."

"OK, sister, we have to be watchful just in case. Can't alert the sheriffs as we have no idea if we are anywhere right. Up ahead some 30 miles is Lone Pine. "Let's hope a motel will be available."

In three hours and three minutes the bicyclers find a motel in Independence, almost across the street from a restaurant. "Well, Sally let's hope they have a room."

They do and with a shower and a hot dinner, Sally and Cooper forget about the man that might had been one of the poachers 3 years ago."

# CHAPTER 12

Cʟɪꜰꜰᴏʀᴅ Bᴀʀɴᴇs, Cᴀʟɪꜰᴏʀɴɪᴀ Hɪɢʜᴡᴀʏ Patrol Officer, stops his patrol car in Olancha. He is buying gum. Twenty-one days of not smoking and Clifford is in need of assistance.

No other customers are in the small grocery store. He speaks up, "Mabel, I need two packs of Juicy Fruit. I'm going on twenty-two days of not smoking. Doc tells me I have to look at thirty days to get over the urge."

"Yeah, Cliff, look at how much weight you've been stacking on your frame. Chewing gum and candy is stretching your clothes."

"You been talking to my wife. She says the same things. She keeps telling me if my quitting smoking is successful the extra food and weight gain will catch me. What's new in your area?"

"Not much Cliff. Wait a minute, I got something for you. I had a brother and sister bicycle in yesterday on a tandem . . ."

"You mean a red tandem bicycle and the girl is blond with a million dollar figure and she is blind?"

"Well, Cliff, with your beady eyes you got it all. Listen, while she was in my store, yesterday, a short built man was also in the store. He kept bumping into this girl. This she told me later. Her brother was with her.

"When they left I went out to see these two leave on their red tandem bicycle. Before they left I could hear her talking to her brother, I think his name was Coop or Cooper.

The girl was saying, "That man kept bumping into me. I'm think he is the same one we caught, I thought she said when he and someone were poaching deer on somebody's ranch up north."

Then she said something like, "These two men were caught by her brother and someone called Meredith."

"It was something like that, then some one came in the store and I had to leave. Does that give you any ideas?" "A bucket full of ideas. I met them when I was returning from the Palmdale meeting. Also a couple of truck drivers, Red an Mac, I know were in 'The Buzzard Cafe.' We were all talking to them. Good kids." "Thanks, but are you going to do something about it?"

"Absolutely nothing. The problem is I can't do anything myself. But I'm going on the horn and call a couple of long haul drivers. I only know them by their first names."

"That bunch drives up down 395 constantly. From those two, we'll have every truck driver plus us and them sheriffs on the look out for the brother and sister. I'm sure she is still wearing those knock out bike clothes."

"Well, I'll tell you, Cliff, she had a outfit on that could stop a parade. Let me know what happens. Another thing, Jimmy, he works across the street. When I mentioned the bicyclers and than short and slightly fat man, Jimmy told me, 'He thinks it's the same man that got into an old blue Volkswagen pickup. "That also may help you guys and that brother and sister duo."

"Oh, Clifford, before you go catching someone, I need some coins for your gum."

Once on the highway, Clifford, the Highway Patrolman, sent out a notice to be on the watch for the two bicyclers and an old blue Volkswagen pickup. The orders were to keep a eye on the bicyclers and report any thing out of place with two bicyclers and/or the blue pickup no matter what. Just keep them under sight control and report to the California Highway Patrol their location.

Cooper and Sally are planning to stop at Manzanar once a camp to house American Citizens of Japanese extraction during the early phases of World War Two, which was now a Federal Monument.

Manzanar is now under control by The United States Federal Park System. Sally and Cooper have another two hours by going through the remains of a black mark on American Citizens.

As they are about half way through their self guided tour, a striking young brunette female ranger notices Cooper and a girl with vision problems.

Cooper was telling Sally what she was feeling. This young Ranger thought she could help.

"Pardon me, sir. May I help you. I noticed the young lady has a sight problem. Can I be your guide?"

Sally replies, "I can't believe it. He did it again." The ranger was puzzled. "Pardon me Miss, I didn't catch that statement." "Oh, that is between my brother and me. I'm blind and he is helping me. "Well, you now have a National Park Ranger as your guide. My name is Ellen and I will be your guide." Sally replies, "This is my brother, Cooper Portage, and he did it again!" "I beg your pardon?" Ellen says. Cooper finally is able to get in the conversation. "My sister is blind and at times her mind wanders. I have been here before and we are bicycling to Yosemite.

"I have told her about this stop so here we are. She will learn more from a young lady than her brother."

Sally tells the ranger, "Watch him, Ellen, he's very smooth." Two hours pass quickly. Cooper checks his watch. He tells Sally,

"Lady, we have to be in high gear to, reach Independence before dark." Ellen questions, "Could that long red two seater bicycle be yours?" "Sure is Ellen." Cooper tells her. "We are biking to Yosemite and once we thought we would be on the road eight days; now, it looks like ten days."

Ellen checks her watch. "I'm off in twenty minutes and I have a small cabin in Independence. Why don't you two stay with me. I'll take the floor and you two the bed. I drive a not so new pickup. Stick your bike in the back as you'll make Independence just before dark. By then every motel is taken. How's that sound?"

"I just don't understand my brother. Every problem he finds, uh, help?" Sally nudges Cooper with her elbow.

Cooper smiles to Ellen. "Because of my rule not bicycling late in the evenings I'm forced to accept your offer, Ellen."

Sally remarks, "When one travels with a pro, act like a pro."

Ellen appears confused with Sally's remark. "What does your sister mean, Cooper?"

"Ellen you just have to accept many of Sally's remarks. I think part of her brain was attached to her eyes.

Regardless of eyes going and maybe her brains as well, we'll accept your kind offer and thank you for asking.

"We have two sleeping bags, and air mattresses. Thank you for the bed, but we'll take the floor.

"Ellen, I'll adjust the bike to fit into your pickup. And we'll stop at a grocery store, and no using your food."

Arriving to Ellen's cabin is a combo of a bedroom and a small bathroom with a shower. There is a one person kitchen joined in, part way, with the combination living room and dining room.

Call it quaint, or small, but it was durable and better than a tent. Cooper noticed an automatic shotgun inside by the front door.

Ellen saw Cooper stare at the gun. "Cooper, that's my first gun. Dad demanded I have protection as I'm alone. Dad and I hunted ducks and pheasants from the time I was allowed to have a hunting license.

"So when Dad saw my living quarters he went back to his car and brought me my first shot gun that I ever owned. That's an automatic 410 shotgun.

"I used that gun until my middle years in high school. Then he bought me a magnum 20 gauge 3 inch shotgun. I left it home.

"I never had to use the gun but living alone and knowing how to use a gun, well it does give me a feeling of protection.

"The government is just getting around our work requiring pistol training. I think our work is, well, that we are at the bottom of the food chain. But the time is coming."

Cooper took over the cooking while the ladies talked. After dinner the ladies conversation continued until Cooper mentioned, "Sally, Ellen has to go to work tomorrow and we, remember what I've said, 'With an early morning start we find less wind to tackle.'"

Sally and Cooper leave another new friend. They are off to Big Pine. Cooper tells Sally, "Say, babe, tonight we make it to Bishop. If we are early we might continue to a camp ground just beyond Bishop. This will be our first mountain pass."

"There's no way to go around it, boss." "I wish it would be possible. Maybe we'll stop in Bishop and get a motel and then tomorrow we'll only have a mountain range to handle.

The following day we'll stop at Lee Vining and the next day we will bike into Yosemite."

"What are you going to do about the string of girls you seem to be collecting, boss?" Sally jabs her finger into Cooper's back.

"No, I'm happy just trying to cultivate Franziska, I think." "Wow, that's the one I thought was the best of the litter, so far." "So you agree with my selection?" "Well I haven't seen them all, sorry about that slip. I mean I haven't heard them all or gotten to know them yet."

"And lady, you won't. Ah, up ahead is a turn out and we'll stop. We have miles to go. I'll walk you through some flowering Cactus plants. Let's keep peddling.

"Say. Aren't there cactus growing in the hot desert, leader?"

'You are right, Sally. However about ten or fifteen years ago a scientific person wanted to check certain desert plants in a higher elevation and he did; then he was taken to another situation and here we are. Certain people are taking care of these desert plants and their growth has caught much interest for scientific people. Let's take a look at these out of the way plants.

Waiting at the Wild Life Scenic area is a blue Volkswagen pickup. Three men are waiting and hoping the tandem bicyclers will stop. They are Adam Hamlin and Scott Tibbs, the two poachers from Dr. Terri's ranch incident. With the two ex-cons, is Mark Ragget. He ain't no good either.

They appear to need help pushing their old pickup while pretending to have a dead battery. This is when Sally and Cooper will bike by.

Adam tells Mark Ragget, "When that red bicycle with the blond gal and that guy bicycle up to you, stop them. Tell them your small pickup has a dead battery. You left the lights on.

"Our pickup will be over the hill. Look at the parking lot. We can't be seen from the highway."

"Just flag them tandem bicyclers and ask for a push. When they arrive we'll finish off the guy and we'll own that blond pussy."

Mark Ragget nods his head. "Sounds good. You two are only giving me thirds?" "Damn right. Scott and I spent 380 days in the slammer because of those two.

"Lets see, they should be coming in about thirty or forty minutes. So get down to the highway and bring them here. No one can see us parked over this hill from the highway. Any questions?

"I still should, at least get seconds." Scott Tibbs answers, "We spent two good years and lots of jacking off in cells. We'll take it easy on that blond. Get down on the highway and give them your best look."

As Coop and Sally bike toward Bishop, Cooper is telling Sally about the types of cactus he is seeing.

"Let's stop here Sister Sally and and I'll guide you to some flowering cactus. I'll hold your hand as these plants have very sharp thorns. Any wandering by you means trouble.'

Trouble, like what, Coop?" "Like sitting on a pin cushion with the pins pointing in the direction your sitting." "You say they are really sharp?" "Right. That's how they survive. Only certain animals and birds survive on cactus. I'm going to stop here alongside the highway. There's no need to bicycle up the grade to see what you can walk among the cactus here."

"Thanks, Coop. Going up a hill to see the scenes that I can't see is kinda dumb on my part. When down at the Look Out Parking Area, the three men exclaim, "Oh, darn, they are stopping down there. Well, let's do it their way. There's hardly any traffic on the highway except them trucks. Let's go and park by that red bicycle."

Adam is driving with Scott in the front seat. Mark Ragget is in the pickup bed.

Adam drives up along side the red tandem bicycle but he points his pickup in the wrong direction. He's pointing away from Bishop. Darn it.

Adam, tell the other two men, "Let's let them get further up the hill. Then, we'll get them. Notice there's a drop off after they get a little higher up, then the land drops off. That's where we'll bang her good and proper."

Mark Ragget, the new man, decides to stay. "Man-o-man, I don't like them cactus. Every time time I'm near them things I get stuck. I'll wait."

Red, the truck driver that Cooper and Sally met in the Buzzard Cafe some days ago is driving his long Semi toward Bishop. He's moving along at a good fair speed of 75 to 80 miles per hour. Red notices an old blue pickup parked off the highway pointing the wrong direction. Along side is the red tandem bicycle. He grabs his radio.

"Mac where are you?" "Just cleared Big Pine, Red." "I just passed the lookout. That red tandem is parked along the road before the Look Out. An old blue German pickup is parked next to the bicycle. Some guy is sitting in the pickup.

I see them two bicyclers way out in the cactus. And two guys are just starting to walk behind them about five or so truck lengths behind the brother and sister. I don't think them bicyclers know anyone is behind them.

"I'm turning around when I can. Something don't smell right. I'll meet you by the red bicycle. Out."

On the two way radio comes the voice of Clifford Brown, The California Highway Patrol Officer. "Listen, you two clowns, don't do something stupid. I'm leaving Bishop with red lights and no siren."

Red comes on the air again, "Hey, Mac, did you hear who just woke up. Our Lone Ranger. Let's make it, the last guy there buys the coffee. Them black and whites can't out run our Reo's."

Over the air comes a voice. "This is Louie, I got a truck full of fish. Count me in."

Red answers, "Did you hear that noise, Mac? That's Louie with the Nose, packing a truck full of fish. Who's doing the BBQ thing?" "Say Mac, did you ever figure out how much fish you could stick up in Louie's nose?" "OK, you guys, we got a project to do. Who thinks they will be first to arrive where the tandem is parked? I can be there in ten minutes. How about you, truckers?"

Mac replies, "Cliff, I'm almost there. I got a 'come along bar' with me?'" "I'm parking it now. My lead pipe is beside me. Shall I wait or go? I'm seeing that two guys are starting to walk up the hill. The bikers are way up. I'm going."

Mark notices another Semi is parking on the west side of 395. Mark is thinking. I gotta get out of here. Another Semi comes to a screeching stop. However, this Semi is pointing toward Bishop.

Mark watches the driver jump from the cab and reaches behind the cab to grab a five foot pipe.

It didn't take long for Mark to decide to leave in the pickup.

Cooper is telling Sally what type of cactus is growing. "Sally, let me take your hand and I'll let you touch it. Feel the sharpness of the needles." "Wow. Those things are sharp, Coop. Why?"

"Sister, in the desert, water in not plentiful. So certain plants developed protection by growing needles. Some plants have tiny needles and others have long needles.

In fact our early Indians used the long needles to kill small animals instead of using large arrows or spears."

"What would happen if someone was to fall in a bunch of this cactus Coop?" "Well, besides the terrific pain, they can't move. Any movement to get out gets more needles into the animal or person.

Sally interrupts Cooper. "Do I hear some talking?" Cooper turns around and notices two men are walking fast up the small trail. In fact they appear to be coming right at them. And not far behind these two men are two coming up fast carrying something like pipes.

Coopers orders, "Sally, don't move we are in a thick cactus patch. Stay where you are. I'm going to see the man who appears to be the leader, and see what he wants. Just stay where you are."

One man tells the other man. "Scott. I'll take that narrow left trail to that gal. I'll grab that sweet ass, she's mine. Take the wide trail and finish the kid."

Sally hears this talking and waits. She's thinking there's trouble coming as she can hear some one walking toward her and swearing. One man is walking closer to her, and swears every time he is poked by a cactus plant.

Sally forces a smile and waits. He's getting close. Sally extends her hand out. The stranger takes her hand, without a strong grip. Sucker, she thought.

Sally makes a quick step forward with her right foot. While holding his right hand, she twists her body and grabs his pants so he is flipped off the trail, face down, and into the cactus plants. The shrieks and yelling stab through the quiet landscape.

Cooper waits for Scott. Scott hears his partner screaming. Now he hears someone behind him running. Looking behind him is a man with a pipe.

Then he turns to the kid in front who he was going to get. That kid is waiting and appears ready for a fight. He has waited too long.

Cooper is thinking, two more steps, come to me, sucker. Scott has a decision to make. Each side of the trail is thick with cactus. The stranger is in front and then this guy is coming fast with something like a pipe coming at me from behind. Who do I take first? Of course, the kid.

Scott Tibbs charges Cooper and receives Coopers best kick on the right, as if Cooper is trying for a 70 yard three pointer. His kick hits Scott's groin bending his body over and he begins screaming.

At the same time as Scott starts to bend over was when Mac Allen, the truck driver, began his swing with the lead pipe that has a leaded two foot tip.

Mac's swing catches this man legs and spins and slams Scott, tumbling, into the thick cactus plants by about six or seven feet. Screaming voices plug off the traffic noise from highway 395.

If any one were standing around, besides Sally, Cooper and Mac Allen, the truck driver, they would have heard giant screams and hollers from two men thrashing in pain.

Cooper waves to Mac as turns to hurry to his sister, Sally. "You, OK?" "Sure, what in the world is going on Coop? There's a lot of yelling. I know one man that tried to get me is, but I hear more screams and yelling." Cooper laughs. "Sally, it's the guys we met in the Buzzard cafe, the two truck drivers, Mac and Red. They came to save us." "What a time to meet! Who are these guys in the cactus? Red replies, "Bad ones. Let's get off the hill. Clifford Barnes, our Highway Patrol watch dog, will be here soon. "What about these guys, Alle? Leave them. They ain't going no where. Oh, look down Mac, Louie just showed up along with Cliff." Cooper wonders out loud, "I think we should stay until the officer shows up?"

Mac mentions, I don't think these guys still asking for help are too far off the road to be under his roof. The sheriffs will handle it. We'll see. Anyway, let's wait till Cliff comes. He's moving up the hill like he has got flat feet. Cliff walks up with hugs and hand shakes go around, especially with Sally.

Red asks, "Aren't you away from your district, Cliff?"

"No. I came to see how our bicyclers are. I would say, you guys and one lovely lady can handle yourselves quite well. I'm glad you all are on our side. You'll have to stay until the sheriff's people arrive and the fire department.

Sally asks, "There was no fire, why the fire department?" Patrol Officer Clifford Barnes smiles, "I told them about your biking outfit. So I guess they are getting all the guys off duty to come here and see you. It sure wouldn't be us boys. This brought out a round of laughter.

Sally thought for a moment then answered, "How did the firemen ever pass their Artificial Resuscitation Classes?"

This brought out a huge laughter from the men. Then Clifford Barnes mentions. "You two may not know it, but the county may have to keep all of you some time to go over your stories. I'll have them, the county, make good arrangements for you to spend the night in Bishop.

"Don't worry about it, I'll handle that and make sure your accommodations are good at no cost and that includes dinner and breakfast as well."

Finally the Sheriff and the County Fire Department arrived.

After consuming time about how the rescue will be handled; first, an entry into the cactus patches had to be made.

So a huge construction tractor with wide tracks had to be found along with a large and wide roller. This took time.

The cactus is packed down using a huge roller pulled by a large track tractor.

The darkness is descending so lights must be added to make a usable entry in recovering the two suffering and crying men.

Then ladders are placed on the crushed cactus. Lights had to be brought in for the rescue as the night is approaching.

Then, it was a wait until four volunteers accepted the job of removing the two cactus wounded, slobbering and crying men.

When the volunteers found out who these men really were, then the work progress slowed down to a crawl.

While the foot dragging rescue work continued, there came a series of worthless verbal suggestions.

No one really wanted to make a fast rescue. The word for the day was: "Let the men suffer for some hours.

And it was hours before the firemen, in their big shining red ladder truck, loaded Sally's tandem bike that the firemen carefully placed on top of the ladders using an excess of padding. Sally strongly demanded it.

Besides, everyone wanted to stay as long as possible to keep their eyes on this girl and her bicycling outfit.

Finally, Sally and Cooper crowd into the huge ladder truck. There were few seats inside and behind the driver. Every fireman volunteered with, "Miss, I have room on my lap."

Upon arriving at the entrance to Bishop, the fire truck driver hits his air horn and siren when they entered town.

One of the firemen mentioned, "Man, this is as big a deal as our "Mule Days" but prettier."

Waiting for them are photographers news reporters and TV people. Sally quietly asks Cooper, "Do you think Franziska will read about this in her paper?"

"Probably not less than a hundred times." "Oh, brother, have you got an ego." "Well, Miss Know It All, what about Eduard?" "OK, smart one. Do you know how well both are thinking about two people, we are just on our bike Sally."

"Well, Coop, we with half-Mexican and Hinez English blood, maybe having another blood dilution or two is needed, except that we really don't know these two people."

Changing the subject, Sally suggests: We'll call the folks now. This gives them a chance to hear our side of the excitement."

Greta, Terri, and Jude, in San Diego, are watching the news while talking. Suddenly there comes a report on the news.

"Two common criminals tried to capture two well-known local young athletes, Sally and Cooper Portage, from San Diego.

A brother and sister on a tandem bicycle were nearly kidnapped near Bishop, California, this afternoon. "Two criminals met the brother and sister team, Sally and Cooper, as they were bicycling with all their supplies strapped on Sally's brand new Tandem bicycle.

They were headed to Yosemite National Park on highway 395 just before entering the city of Bishop.

"Sally and Cooper Portage, stopped to smell and look at a huge patch of cactus off route 395 by a couple of hundred yards.

"Sally Portage, a future swimming Olympian, was selected by these two men for a kidnap.

"Her brother, Cooper Portage and an All American Soccer player and a third string All American football player, was to be killed by these two men.

"It was a very bad choice by these ex cons. These criminals are now in a secured federal hospital being treated for massive cactus injuries. "One has a shoulder dislocation from meeting Sally Portage, who is blind, when she flipped this man, end over end into the cactus patch.

"The other ended up with abdominal injuries along with two broken legs, and massive groin injuries and being impaled with hundreds of cactus. He received these injuries when Sally's brother, Cooper Portage and a truck driver, Mac Allen went into action on the trail in the middle of a large cactus patch.

According to Max Allen, the truck driver, and Cooper Portage: Cooper used his famous kick and then with the swinging of a lead pipe from Mac Allen, the truck driver, their quick actions solved the problem.

"So much for a kidnapping murder attempt." "Both criminals have ended up with hundreds of cactus needles all over their bodies and possible severe eye injuries and life threatening infections.

One man received severe groin injuries from receiving a kick from our All American soccer player and an outstanding football kicker, and extra pointer kicker.

Cooper's kick was followed by Max Allen, a teamster swinging his lead pipe at the legs of Allen.

Cooper Portage described his actions as, "I was running back to help Sally. When this guy grabbed Sally's hand. Suddenly he's thrown head over heels into a thick patch of cactus.

"Then the second man was running right at me. I turned to face him and quickly decided to try a 70 yard punt. Mac, the truck driver, swung his lead pipe at the same time I'm giving this fellow my 70 yard boot.

"We couldn't have planned this better. That fellow went into an end over end flight into those cactus plants, yelling all the way. He made a beautiful arms out and face down belly flop in the cactus."

"Mac and I left this fellow well planted, along with Sally's man also screaming in the cactus gardens. It was very loud screaming so we three left. None of us wanted to step one foot in the cactus.

"The two truck drivers and Clifford, the Highway Patrolman, we first met in the Buzzard Cafe three days ago.

All of us decided to let the fire department handle the removal of those men."

"The television announcer continued: "According to the Medical staff in Bishop, The force of the injuries will confine the men for a least a month.

"The cactus wounds may be more dangerous due to infections all over their bodies. Each man will lose at least, one eye and chances are both eyes."

Jude stands up and turns the television off. "Greta, we had better pull the plugs on our telephones if we're going to Yosemite tomorrow."

"Jude, what was the name of that girl Sally said for us to pick up in Palmdale? I'll call her now for directions. Maybe she caught the news.

Greta returns after talking to Sally. "Jude, her name is Franziska Zimmerman. I wrote down her address and phone number. Maybe she watched the news.

"Sally was very positive about having Franziska come along with us. I think Sally made the offer. As I understand, Cooper is unaware about this plan."

Terri McGill walks over to the kitchen drain board and returns with 3 water glasses of homemade wine. She gives a glass to Greta and Jude.

"Let me make this toast to this father and mother who are now together. What a family you have. Two kids as sharp as tacks, hitting all the keys in their young life. And to Sally who thinks she found a girl, hopefully, a wife for Cooper, her biggest supporter, and perhaps a sister-law."

Jude returns from his telephone call. "This girl, rather a lady, will have a degree in Psychology in May next year. Franziska, indicated she will go for a Masters degree all the while she was crying. She told me she watched the news on television.

"When I asked her to come with us to Yosemite, she cried again. I think for once Cooper will be surprised. Yes, this will be a first. I can hardly wait."

# CHAPTER 13

Jude, Greta, Terri, and Franziska had driven to Yosemite entering from the Fresno side. They pass the three water falls, and the fourth, Yosemite Falls, almost right next to Yosemite Village Hotel.

Jude is standing at the reservation desk of the Village Hotel. He has a copy of a reservation for two rooms and will request one more.

He waits. Finally the clerk returns and and says Mr. Portage, "Your reservations are not here." The clerk is smiling.

Jude eyes the young man. "I have copies of my complete reservations."

"They don't count, sir." Jude digs in this wallet looking for his reservation copy. The smiling clerk is upsetting Jude. Now the clerk says, "I'm sorry, sir, but your reservations have been upgraded and added to. Your three rooms will overlook the Merced River and you have three decks. Then, you have one at the Ahwahnee Hotel, free gratis."

"Who did that? We are not supposed to be here, uh Ahwahnee? Are you kidding me or are you sure?"

"Let me tell you. Your son and daughter are considered heroes from all the people in the valley, especially the bicyclers. And we have a bunch of bicyclers, from workers to rangers. Every one of them is smiling at what your son and daughter did."

"Those two will be spending the nights at the Ahwahnee. Your three rooms, here, will be over looking the river."

Jude returns to Terri, Franziska and Greta, "Terri, some time I have to have a meeting with you describing how two young adults can flip through their life free and easy."

"Me? Mr. Portage? I'm as confused as anyone in this room." Terry turns to Franziska, "Maybe you understand how these bicyclers get into these problems and come out smiling?" "Me? Dr. Terri, and you with a Doctoral degree? I with three classes in, and one go and a Master's degree on the line. Then a Doctoral, hopefully. The Master's coming up. But I'll sure ask when I get back to school.

She continues, "Nothing, I have ever read mentioned how certain people can evade or sail through sudden mental and physical problems like the Portage's brother and sister did.

"Maybe we are looking at it the wrong way, Dr. McGill? It might be the father and mother that we should consider."

Terri is smiling, Franziska you hit it. That's the clue. You will go a long way in your field.

No sooner had Greta and Jude moved into a double room with Terri and Franziska, when a knock came on their door. A bell hop in a green uniform came in holding a tray with two bottles of wine and cheese and crackers.

He tells the Greta and Jude, "This is compliments of the management. We understand, the younger generation heroes, Sally and Cooper, will hit the floor of the valley this evening. We'll keep you all informed every fifteen minutes on their arrival."

Jude looks at Greta. "Did we miss something raising those two? If we can figure it out how they do it, we can bottle it and make a fortune."

Franziska suggests, "Include the influence of your world trips, Mr. Portage. That may be the answer. You did it. Now tell us how you did it"?

"Sure. Find one intelligent woman, soak her in the business ethics of her husband, and send him around the world numerous times. Keep him moving. Then, remember the wife who stays home with two active kids. She became the maker of laws and the judge and jury. Mrs. Portage had the toughest job. That's my guess."

Jude looks at his wife. "Greta, I have to ask you this: "Before we left to come to Yosemite, I was told that my two partners wives met with our attorney, and established a new rule.

"I wasn't in town when this rule was made. And according to the agreement: Our work hours will begin at eight in the morning and end at five in the afternoon.

"If there are any extensions created on extra time, it requires one hundred dollars payment to the three wives for each hour later or before our set time.

"The three partners will pay the other partner's wives one hundred dollars per every hour over five in the afternoon or before eight in the morning.

"According to our attorney, that statement was demanded by one or more wives. I have a feeling you had a hand in that ruling."

"Who, little me?" Later in the day Sally was on the telephone talking with her mother.

Her last sentence was, "He's so confident and right; this will surprise the smart brother I have."

At six in the evening. Greta, Terri, Franziska, and Jude are out on the deck talking. It was such a warm evening. Then, the telephone rings."

Jude answers. "Great, we'll be right down, but remember I have three ladies. Do you understand that statement?"

"Hah, Hah, So do you. I'll get the gals out in a couple of minutes. Thank you and I'll see you down there."

Greta asks, "What was that about and three ladies?" "We are wanted downstairs now. Let's go." Franziska says, "I believe Cooper is here with Sally, let's go." Theses four people didn't think the elevator would be fast enough.

The hotel rumbled with four people going down the stairs.

The first words they heard were, "Coop, we have a gift for you." Cooper and Sally are standing by their Tandem bicycle and were almost knocked over with a sudden crying of Franziska, who grabbed Cooper and locked her hands around his neck.

Finally Cooper is able to, slightly on his part, ask, "Franziska, what a wonderful surprise. I was hoping you would show up. I should have known it was Sally who planned it."

"Cooper, I never thought I could say this to any man, I don't ever want lose you."

Cooper stops kissing Franziska to say, "And you never will. It's Sally. You two lovely conniving ladies. I love you, both."

Greta breaks into the conversation. "Shall we clean up and have dinner, our first dinner all together?"

"Wait Mom," Sally and I have to check in at the Ahwahnee Hotel. We need to clean up and change our clothes. I hope some one packed some clothes. Do I hear a yes?"

"Yes, dear son, your old Mother packed yours and your sister's clothes. The blue suitcase is yours. What you need should be in the suit case."

Franziska speaks up. "I hope, Cooper, you have a shaving kit ready to use tonight?"

Jude laughs and slaps Cooper on the shoulder, "Well, son, welcome to the land of women."

Suddenly four voices of the women came to the defense of Jude's remark.

After an excellent dinner at the Ahwahnee Hotel, the entire Portage group walked back to the Riverside Hotel. On the way back, the night was warm with a clear sky.

By now many visitors have heard the news about the experiences of the brother and sister. Some people stop the Portage group and congratulate them.

"Oh, such a dangerous act you two performed on those dangerous men."

"I can't believe any one would bicycle from San Diego to Yosemite. And with all those speeding cars and trucks on the highway. You said you weren't bothered by that crazy traffic."

And so it went. Jude placed his hotel key in the lock then exclaimed, "Who forgot to lock the doors?"

Greta remarked, Honey, I believe it was you." Jude remarks, "I thought I left some lights on. Can some one find the gizmo to turn on the light?" As they enter the room, sitting in a chair in the middle of the room is a man with his left hand holding an old western 45 pistol with the hammer pulled back.

The man smiles. "Well, come and grab a seat so I can see all of you. You, blonde, shut the door."

Cooper says, "She can't, she's blind." "OK, then, you in the slacks, shut the door now. I have a nervous finger." Greta slowly shuts the door. Then turns and asks, "What's going on?

What do you want?" "Oh, you don't know? Let me tell you. Your son and daughter nearly killed my two friends the other day. So I come for a little revenge, and a little action with that blind girl. I'm surprised now that I have more women than I can handle at once.

"But, being the man I am, I'll stretch it out and make it last all night. How does that saying go in the book? Yeah. My cup runs over."

"In case some one wants to make a move, this 45 carries six bullets. There's enough for everyone. One bullet hitting one person will knock against the wall, so don't try to be a hero, it's over buddy."

"I want everyone to sit on the floor.

"No chairs. Franziska stands up and grabs her purse and starts to walk toward the man with the gun.

"Hey, lady, get your sweet ass back on the floor." Franziska barks at the man, "I've got to go to the bathroom in a hurry." "No way. Sit down. Piss on the floor." Franziska steps closer to the man with the pistol. "I just told you I have to go now, can't you understand that? It's my period. You want to see? I'll show you." She moves to stand on the man's right side. With her purse in her left hand she reaches in her open purse. "I'll show you now. Her hand goes into her purse.

This man leans back, and perhaps he doesn't want to see. Franziska whips out a five inch knife handle with a four inch shining blade and sticks it right into his stomach with a twist with her right hand holding his pistol pointing down.

This is quickly followed by a nearly complete slash to his throat leaving his head dangling to one side and blood surging on the room floor.

Greta and Terry gave out with screams. Sally grabs Cooper who is sitting next to her on the floor. "What's going on, Coop?"

Cooper tells Sally, "Don't move." He jumps up and with two steps he grabs Franziska and holds her tight to his body.

She is shaking and crying saying, "I've never done anything like this. I'm feeling like I'm going to faint. Honey, hold me."

Jude snaps off some bed covers, telling Terri, "Get the hotel people and the rangers."

"All of us go in the next room, now. You too, Coop, and help Franziska.

Jude grabs a tablet and some pens on a stand next to the telephone stand and takes them into the next room. "Everyone start writing what you saw and heard. Quickly, before the rangers arrive. Remember what was said and how you saw Franziska handle the problem.

Cooper is holding Franziska on his lap, while seated on a large stuffed easy chair. She is crying and shaking.

Cooper keeps telling her, "Honey, you did the right thing. You saved all our lives."

In between sobs, she says, "But I just killed some one. Please keep holding me."

"How about holding you forever, as my wife." "Are you proposing to me in this terrible situation when I just killed a man?" "Darling, I don't want to lose you now or forever." There's more sobbing. "I'll marry you, but hold me." Terri walks into the room where every one of the Portage clan are seated, still somewhat in shock.

She announces, "I have a bottle of Single Malt Scotch. Who wants a hit?"

Franziska, in a weak shaking voice, as she holds a tight grip around Cooper's neck, and in a trembling voice says, "Two good shots over here, Terri, for me and my man, please."

It took time to unravel the whole picture of how Mark Ragget was able to find what rooms the Portages had and left unlocked.

A guest doctor suggests, "I believe Miss Zimmerman should be taken to a hospital for a check up."

Franziska was adamant. "No way! I want my man with me and all my friends with me, especially my man. If I go, he has to go with me."

So Cooper, that night, sat in a large easy chair, holding his wife to be, throughout the night.

Franziska would doze off then suddenly wake up and say, "Honey, I never ever thought I would kill a man." Cooper would reply, "Listen, my lovely lady, you were the only one that was in the position to save us all. You, my dear, you are a keeper." "Just keep on remembering that statement. I am still going to carry a knife in my purse." Cooper asks, "Why in the world were you thinking of carrying a small dagger in your purse?" "A girl should always carry protection. Did you notice that the knife was not a switch blade. That's illegal to have." "My Dad, wait tell you meet him; he showed me many ways to protect myself. One was how to use a knife for my protection.

He was a Green Beret and a thirty year man in the army. When he was stationed in Germany on some training project, he met my mom. "Dad has drilled me in many ways to protect myself. My knife was not a switch blade. That saves a lot of legal questions, just like yesterday evening. Those rangers, sure caught that fast. What are your plans, Mr. Portage?"

"OK, my first plan is that I'm taking Sally to USC early in August to meet her swimming coaches before she enters college. Would you like to go with me and Sally to USC? Hint, Hint?"

"I'm on my Master's at USC, Mr. Portage. So Sally is going to USC. So am I. School is starting soon.

"Then, if you'll drive me home, as I have to get my car then drive back to USC. Isn't that a lot of driving? Of course, Cooper, you'll need your car or is that a truck I hear your family kid you about."

Franziska suggests, "Honey, we'll both graduate in the end of May. "We'll finish our Master's at the same school?"

"I don't think so. I'm on a fast program working for my lead instructor. He keeps shoving more work on me. I even have freshmen entering class to teach this next year.

# CHAPTER 14

THIS WAS SOME SUMMER when Cooper met Franziska's family. Mr. Robert Zimmerman is called by all his friends and family, as 'The Colonel,' and he was. He's a large muscular man that still works out.

When Cooper was introduced to 'The Colonel', Cooper was sized up very quick.

"So, you're the player with the toe. Been reading about your skills at Poly. Going Pro, Cooper?"

"No, sir. By graduating in May, I'll have my degree in architecture and may pick up an engineering degree sometime along the line. It will be probably about two more years to polish off the engineering phase, uh, "Well, I've been offered part time architect work with a national company rechecking some work this company is handling in San Luis Obispo. It's really more engineering work. I'll run it in with my class work."

"From what I hear, there's a wedding in the picture." Colonel, I'm sorry, you did not get it from me." "I understand you have been around. You know the drill with women. They are tough cats to keep a secret, Coop." "Colonel, you're correct. Especially when they carry a knife in their purse and know how to use it.

"Fritzy was a hard pupil to teach. But I guess her training worked. "You don't mind me calling you, son, do

197

you? Up to now I've been living in a sorority house. So, Son, let's join the ladies for dinner.

All the way to San Diego, inside Cooper's reconditioned 30 year-old pickup, the discussions centered on living together while finishing their Masters; and hopefully, in the same University; and the date for the wedding?"

Franziska points out, "Honey," and she leans heavy on Honey. "I know my school has so many engineering degrees. Why are you so positive to pickup another degree where you are?"

"Fritzy, I want to be the best architect there is. I would rather work on large buildings."

"Well, that means traveling, honey. My Dad did a lot of traveling. It seemed each year I was in a new school and had new friends. One time it was five new schools and five years of tears. Some were American schools usually in some foreign country. I can speak some six languages besides English. My toughest was when I had moved to a new school in mid-term. It was very hard to adjust. "I just don't know what I would do if I find myself constantly packing and unpacking. What about your business future?"

"You are right. I have seen Mom almost beside herself with Dad's traveling and the long weeks and months of not having her husband around and, also, it was the same with Sally and me.

"OK, my love, this is my promise. So far, with my grades I can almost pick just about anywhere I will work and live. We'll have a selection committee pick who I'll work for and where we'll live."

"Who will be on the committee, Coop?" "Just you and I. I'll give you two votes to my one and one half, fair enough?" "Cooper, why did you say that?" "Just because, when I first met you I knew some how that we would get married. Somehow Sally figured it out. Don't ask me how, but she did. Sally was the one that had Dad call you. So you were fingered from the start. Love you, dear."

"You better remember that always. Now, I'm in USC and you are at Poly. What's half way between?"

"This is my last year. If you're thinking we will live half way between, then, it's Santa Barbara. There's traffic and more traffic. Suppose we get married after our graduation?"

"Coop. How can I hold you to that promise?" Cooper smiles. Then answers, "I think I can. Sally suggested I should have this. He reaches into his front left pocket and brings out an emerald cut diamond ring. "Fritzy, would you consider this ring as a promise of marriage after our graduations?"

Franziska is shocked. She's holding the ring with tears rolling down her face. Her mouth is open, but she's not saying a word.

Cooper smiles, takes the ring out of her hand, and starts to slide it back into his pocket.

With a strong voice, Cooper has never heard, Franziska demands, "What in the world are you doing, Mr. Cooper Portage-Santana? That's my ring now and forever! Put it on my finger or I'll scratch your brown eyes out."

Cooper is laughing so hard he has tears.

"Wow. You're one tough lady." He rubs his eyes and now asks, "Honey, may I have your left hand. I'll place the ring on your correct finger, if you wish." "Not, I wish. I want it now. Is there a history with this ring? It is such an unusual cut." "Yes. My great grandfather was a jockey on flat saddle thoroughbreds as well as carts with Pacers and Trotters. He raced under the name,

'The Rube'. One time, for four years, he was the "all around jockey" in United States. "He wanted to marry my great grandmother, this was in, I believe, Kansas. I don't remember or was told how she ever met a jockey. I think one of 'Grams' brothers knew Ruben as he also raced in the carts.

"My great grandmother was a very religious person and told Ruben that he had to quit racing for money if he wanted to marry her, and he did. This is the ring he gave her Franziska, with tears still rolling down her face, and holding this precious ring, she says in a cracked voice, "Why, Coop, do I love you? I'm going to spend the rest of my life trying to find out why I love you so. Please place the engagement ring on my left hand."

Sally is packing up ready to enter USC.

"Gee Mom, all the gals and boys on the race team were so helpful to me."

"Was Eduard there?"

"Oh sure. He was very helpful. Do you remember when we first went there he had most of the swim team around and he even found that dorm for me, and Katie to be my roommate?"

"Sally, I thought he did an excellent job getting you introduced all around the campus. Is there anything between you two?"

"Nothing yet. He's just a nice man and a gentleman, so polite. All the girls think he's special and can't figure out how I already knew him when you first took me there."

"You told them?" "No." What do your coaches think about your times in swimming?" Coach Knox told me to practice hard. He said, "We can drop two seconds off my time on each of my sprints and I can make the Olympic team next year. Wow. How's that Mom?"

"Sounds great, but don't forget your school work. That's more important.

"What time is Eduard showing up today?" "Four o'clock, promptly." "Sally, do you realize that your friend is driving from Sacramento to San Diego to pick you up, then is driving to Santa Monica, another three hours depending on traffic?'

"Yep. That's what he wanted." "I know he is a splendid young lad. He said what in his plans were to be after graduation, and he mentioned law when we were touring the campus of USC."

"It's Law and Eduard has added Sociology. He wants to be able to handle witnesses that lie, that's what he wants."

"So. Eduard will have another year in school by taking Law and another major?" asks Greta.

"Perhaps. Just like Coop. The way he talks about it sounds like Cooper will spend his life going to college. He hates it and loves it. He told me his lead professor is one tough person. Some of his class mates dropped out. They couldn't stand the professor."

"Sally, your brother, at times, will take the roughest road rather than the smooth highway. Now, do you understand Eduard is driving from Sacramento to San Diego some 400 or so miles? Then he picks you up in the afternoon and drives to Santa Monica to your college, USC.

"That's a lot of driving for one person." "Mom, that is what he wanted." "OK. As I understand Eduard will be here shortly." "Four the afternoon. He is very punctual, Mom." "OK. It's nearly four now." "Mom, Sally lets out a squeal. That's his car. Eduard is here. Open the front door, Mom." "Be a lady and please let him ring the bell." "But I want to see him now."

"Wait." He steps on the porch, then the door bell rings. Sally was standing next to the front door, opens the door and jumps right on Eduard who catches her, then a long kiss follows. Then, another longer kiss comes.

Finally Greta asks, "Won't you come in Eduard and bring that person in your arms as well."

"Mom, all I was doing was giving Eduard a welcome."

"Sally. Do you want me to say something else? Untangle yourself and both of you come on in. Dad will be here shortly, Eduard.

"I have a light lunch made. You must be tired with all the miles it you took to get here.

Greta shuts the front door after Eduard and Sally untangle them selves. How was the trip here, Eduard?"

"Wow. The traffic coming and going in San Diego is something. Your weather is great, but the traffic is something else.

Greta tells the two, "Grab a seat I have a light lunch ready for every one. I just heard a car door slam, it's Jude."

Jude entered the dining room giving a kiss to Greta and Sally. He shakes hands with Eduard.

"So this is the man our daughter has been telling us about a couple weeks ago from her experience at USC.

"Did you fly or drive here, Eduard?" "No. I drove here." "From Sally's description of you, I thought you had wings." Then came two loud voices, "Dad, please."

Jude continues. "Well, Eduard, I have to get to work and I know you have some distance to travel this afternoon, so let's join the ladies the for a light lunch if there ever was a light lunch."

Some tears were apparent in Jude's eyes. Greta is dabbing her eyes with a napkin. Sally is buckled in the front seat and waves a good bye.

Jude remarks, "There is nothing like a daughter in love.

It's five in the afternoon and Sally and Eduard are off to USC in Santa Monica. Sally is strapped in the seat next to the side window.

About two miles have passed. Sally suggests, Eduard, please find a spot to stop, please.

He is surprised. "OK. Right up ahead is a park. I'll stop there." Sally unbuckles her safety strap. Then she slides over to the middle seat and re-straps herself. "I just thought I could be closer to my driver. Ok, lets go. "Are you tired of driving from your home to my home?"

"No. Sally. I do enjoy your company." Sally has placed her left hand on Eduard's thigh. "What are your plans this evening. Are you going the distance or stopping before?" "Well, I did make a reservation at a motel on the beach close to Santa Monica. We should be there in a hour and a half." "We are spending the night in a motel tonight?" "I have made, also, a reservation for a late dinner. I knew we could not leave your house early in the afternoon. If our room has two beds you will want one and I'll take the other bed."

"Suppose, Eduard, they have only one bed. Then what?" "I'll sleep on the floor." "You. What? Did I hear you right, Eduard, did I hear you right? You are going to sleep on the floor, like a dog? "Eduard, did you have any sex education in your school?"

"Twice." "You mean you flunked the course and had to take it over again?"

"For heaven's sake. Sally. My first was when some churches wiggled into our school to teach sex to the junior class.

"We read stories on what happens to girls and boys when the girl becomes pregnant; also, a lot of stuff like that. Here is a good one. We learned the correct way to dress and undress in a closet." I haven't told you, my parents are medical doctors.

"When I told my folks one night at the dinner table what lessons I was learning with regard to sex and what it covered, I thought my folks were going to declare war.

"They marched right into our school trustee meeting along with other parents. So my folks were allowed to have, at home, classes on information about sex. They had to keep records.

"It was so well received that other parents sent their kids to our house for lessons, and many parents came and stayed to learn.

"I've been told that many schools now follow my folk's lesson plans. So your question was?"

"Our sleeping arrangement and that one of us is sleeping on the floor. Before you answer. Do you have any protection with you?"

"What, what do you mean, protection?" "If you took the class it's rubbers, those flexible, stretchable, birth control non-reusable male protection. Rubbers are usually discussed in men's toilet facilities. Now do you understand what I'm driving at? It's you, honey. Are you prepared tonight?"

Eduard had slowly parked his car in front of a motel. He's laughing and holding his handkerchief dabbing his eyes."

"All I can say is yes, yes, and yes. I've been prepared for two years, but never found the lady I really desired to have sex with. I've not done any back seat events, no pickups, or paid girls? Never.

"So, for years I have carried three condoms in my wallet and a small box in my bag. Is your question answered?"

Sally had removed her safety belt. She grabs Eduard and with many kisses she says. How are we going to be listed on the registering book at the motel?"

"My dearest Sally, I know you have gloves, wear them and I will register us as Mr. and Mrs. Eduard Brunner and use my home address. What other information do you need?'

"Wait till we are alone in our room, tonight. Let's get going and I'll train you as the husband I always wanted. Let's get to the motel you reserved."

Registering was no problem. Before entering their room Sally suggested, "Can you carry me into the room?

"I've been practicing for months to do this." Sally is now sitting on the bed. She mentions, First things first. I have to use the bathroom facilities first. You can use them second. Then we can take a shower together, period. Then, we'll dress and have dinner. After that it's the bedroom and lights out.

"This is my first and you said this is your first. Bring your box with you to the bed. We'll use it after dinner. Keep the three in your wallet. I've got to use the toilet. Please show me."

At six in the morning Eduard slowly awakes. In front of him is Sally's back, less clothes. Eduard rubs his eyes. That was some night.

He moves closer to Sally and wraps one arm around Sally. She stirs. Slowly, she moves on her back. One hand goes searching and finds Eduard. Sally asks, "Honey, how was your night?"

I had a dream. I was with the most beautiful young lady. Did you know when I first met you at the campground, I fell in love with right then? When I got home I told my folks I found the girl of my dreams. And you turned out to be more than I expected."

Sally brings her hand around Eduards head and pulls his to hers for more kisses. Then she says, I hope I wasn't too loud last night." "Nobody hammered on the walls."

"Eduard, don't move. Wait. Lead me to the toilet, please. "There's enough time to spend a week here. Let's get up. I'll hold your hand." As Sally stands up., Eduard tells Sally, "You have the best figure ever, When wearing a bathing suit, you will have guys staring everywhere." "Hmmm. Save it. Take me to the toilet and wait. Then I want to work up to a big breakfast with my man."

Franziska is at USC. "Say, lady, how would you like to go back to Santa Catalina Island this long weekend?"

"What's wrong, Coop. I thought you told me you were tied up all weekend."

"I did. Dr. Fredor Sokolov just tossed his keys on my desk saying,

'Take Franziska and get out of here." "I'll pick you up early tomorrow morning. I have three days off. It's the same for you." "Coop, that's great. Is that the cabin we used before?" It's the same one. Can you flag down Sally and Eduard?" "Woo. I don't know. As I remember there's only two bedrooms." "Well, one of them can sleep on the couch." "I think they are beyond that."

"How would you know?" "We can always ask."

"Who's we?" "She's your sister." "Well, their are certain things a brother can ask and this is one you don't ask. You ask." Finally Franziska accepts. I'll call Sally. On Friday morning at 10, you can pick me up at the Campus Coffee Shop 2. I know it's a long drive. See you, love." Friday morning at 0930 Cooper is holding down a table in USC's Coffee Shop 2. He notices Eduard walking by. "Ambulance Chaser, over here."

"Coop. What in the world you doing here? Are you out of your reservation?"

"Slightly. Franzi and I are planning to spend the long weekend on Catalina Island. My lead prof. has a nice two bedroom house on the island.

"Franzi and I have used it before. We wondered if you and Sally would go with us."

"I don't see any problem. We occasionally slip off to the desert. The island sounds great. I've never been there. We are done for this week. There's no swim practice for us.

We were talking about hitting the desert again. The island sounds better."

If you were counting girls or young ladies in the number 10 class, the two girls walking into this coffee shop would be over the 10 grade.

Sally and Franziska, holding hands, have just entered the coffee shop. There were kisses and hugs. So the four will be spending the long weekend on the island. Sally asks, "Do they have tours that we can take to see the island?"

Cooper replies, I think we boys might free up you two ladies for a brief look around, that is, if we have time."

Sally lets out, "Cooper, you have a dirty mind."

After starting the fall semester at USC, Sally has ripped up the college swimming marks of the 50, 100, and the 200 dashes. She rules the dashes.

Sally has been mentioned to have a corner on the swimming dashes. Even though she is blind, her races in her conference are no competition. But she might cross in another lane. She has never crossed another lane in races.

One girl in Montana has similar times. So the finals to represent the United States in the coming Olympics promises to be pushing aside the world mark in dashes.

With this comes the unusual fact that this swimmer is blind and owns or has tied two world swimming dash records. On campus Sally is known and not just as that blind girl. But she is our champion swimmer.

Eduard has become Sally's guard and driver, for the queen of USC and the swimming world. The National finals are in August in Missoula, Montana.

Two couples are caught in the late spring swimming trials. Eduard has his California State license tests.

Cooper had been assigned a project by Dr. Fredor Sokolov two years before and he is sill on the project.

Franziska has been upset with the 200 miles separation, so she was able to transfer to Cal Poly.

Not having seen Cooper for three days, Franziska marches into Coopers lab. "Is this where you spend time that should be my time with you?

"Honey, this very important. My future rests on this project." "What is it?"

"I don't know."

"What? You are working on a project and you don't know what it is?" Why work on it?"

"Thousands of architects and engineers will appreciate what I have accomplished when I finish."

"Wait a minute, Mr. Portage. You are working on something, your not sure what it is that these people you just mentioned would want, but you don't know what it is?"

"Am I missing something?" "A whole lot." "When can we get together, alone, at the ocean or the mountains for a weekend? "Gee, Franzi, I don't know. This project is taking my time and don't forget I have two classes to teach. "One is on Monday, Wednesday, and Friday. The other class is Tuesday, Thursday, and Saturday." Franziska stares at Cooper. "I transferred to Poly to finish my Masters and spend time with you. Yeah, some time is right. That's what I get. Some time which is nothing. If you are coming home to our cottage this weekend, maybe I'll see you then. Good day."

Sally is in here her last days before the finals in Missoula, Montana. Her three events the 50, 100, and the 200 meters she owns. However, there's a girl in Montana who has almost similar times as Sally's.

The finals begin on Monday coming up, today is Thursday.

Cooper has just received a special and highly secret computer that required a protected area. Cooper is under the impression that it belongs to our government. This was handled by Dr. Fredor Sokolov.

Now Cooper's time is 24 hours living with, and operating this computer in complete secrecy.

The operator of this computer in this building has only two keys to all doors, and the last door where this 'some thing or other' is kept bolted to the floor. Off to one side is a toilet and an old army cot.

Now this is Cooper's work station which had him captive for the last eight days. Today, Franziska has entered this building, and even the floor where Cooper works. Now she enters Cooper's work area, and this was a surprise.

"Honey, how did you get here?" "I just followed my Dad's teaching." "Fritzy, You didn't hurt anybody did you?" "No. I came to ask you, are you coming with the family or with Eduard to the finals this Monday in Missoula?" "I can't see any way out. I'm just about to crack open what I have been working on for two or more years." Mr. Portage, I know that. Are you going to see your lovely sister crack the records and become the first blind swimmer, or blind anything, to compete in the Olympics?"

Cooper shakes his head. I understand very well what Sally is going to do, but I'm at the very edge of cracking open in the fields of Electronics, Physics, Atom smashers, and any one I missed, a new, out of this world, blasting old formula's, something entirely so new, that it is impossible to understand. No, I can't see my sister race. Sorry."

Franziska spins and hits the entry door knocking, Dr. Fredor Sokolov, against the wall without an apology.

Dr. Sokolov straightens his jacket. "Well, Cooper, do I sense a family problem?"

Cooper grabs Dr. Sokolov and straightens his jacket and pulls the Doctor to this new computer/machine. "Look here, Doctor, We did it. There it is. You led me to the source. You did it!"

Dr. Sokolov places his right arm around Cooper. You, I suggest young man after three days of checking, back filling, redoing, then this secret ; you, my associate, will blast this to world. You will be on the front page of every science book. You'll be making speeches to every college. And I may say, they pay well."

"Wait a minute Dr. Sokolov. You are in this with me." "No way, Coop, (for the first time Dr. Fredor Sokolov had ever used the name "Coop or Cooper in over two years.) "If I were you, I'd run this subject back and bring it forward and do this a couple of times. Keep your records secure. "I'll be "back Monday morning. This is still a secret between you and me with a big period."

# CHAPTER 15

After three sleepless days and nights, Cooper worked without a shower, shave, and was in the same clothes before and after his week of ten days of effort.

Monday at ten in the morning Cooper finishes his project. He slumps into an old wooden chair just when Dr. Sokolov enters this hideaway room.

"Partner." He just called Cooper a partner, "How did it go?" "Exactly the same." "Don't you have a sister trying out for the Olympics swimming.

Coop?" "Yes, this afternoon in Montana." Dr. Fredor Sokolov replies, "Stay right here, I'll be right back." In ten minutes he returns. "Cooper, get yourself into that monstrosity of a painted pickup and get to the airport. "A red and yellow plane will fly you to Missoula. Don't delay. I wish your sister good luck. "I'll handle the project in your name. Go as you are. Get out of here."

Cooper parks his eye catching pickup at the airport and walks to the standard fence. Now he notices a new red and yellow painted twelve passenger jet. He's thinking, How did he do it?

Cooper pushes through the crowd who are watching and opens the gate. The crowd gave him some room. Cooper thought, without a shower or a shave in ten days I must smell like a bum. Now I'm getting a ride in a jet.

A sliding step comes out and a flashy flight attendant with a short red and yellow skirt, motions to Cooper to hurry. Upon a closer look, she has everything above her short skirt somewhat covered but they bounce.

Once in the plane it now begins to taxi. The flight attendant shows Cooper the inside of the jet. "Here's a private room and if you want there's a shower, and I think you should soap and shave. You can stay in here or pick a seat. Take your shower when we level off. Meanwhile until that time, catch a seat and buckle in." "I'll let you know when and if you need help on anything, a wink will do. I give great massages in that single room for two people. We are turning on the run way. Buckle yourself in now."

They came down the runway and then straight up and up. Cooper glances at his watch. It's 11:35. He's thinking that there's no way to see Sally swim."

The flight attendant returns as soon as the jet leveled off. "Shower and shave time, okay?" She walked the short distance it was a smooth walk. She told Cooper, "My middle name is Estra, that's short for Concupiscent.

Cooper smiles. She just told me she's erotic. Well, she's got the wrong man. When I see Dad, I'll ask him about Estra.

Once inside the private bathroom she points to the shower. "I'm great for helping in the shower room. Notice a pull down and single padded bed for two over there. If you need help showering or a rub down, that comes with the flight in my cockpit."

Cooper explains, "My wife is waiting for me, thank you anyway." "Maybe you may want to try my style. It never fails with a passenger."

"Sorry miss, I 'm going to shower and shave. I don't need help, but thanks for the offer."

From 1120 to 1240 the jet is setting up for a landing. It was smooth. Cooper was ready to unload when Mary Bell turns Cooper around and gave him wet deep kiss. Then she drops the steps.

As Cooper leaves, Mary Bell tells Cooper, "I'm still just thinking about you and what we could have done. "Next time I'll show you what I was going to give to you, many times."

At the parking lot a number of taxis wait. One taxi intrigued Cooper's eyes. It was a much older taxi but well polished.

The driver is black. Cooper had the feeling that some one was saying.

"Take this taxi."

So Cooper walked past the 1 and 2 year old taxi's to climb in the front seat of this 10 year old highly polished black painted taxi.

Where are you going, Captain, Sir?" "Where the Olympic swimming events are being held." Now Cooper notices, the driver has a somewhat round rock between his thighs. And according to his taxi license, his name is, "Dusty" Mac Greager." "So, your first name is Dusty?" "Yep. Got it as a kid. Only black kid in my high school." "OK, Dusty. Why the rock behind your legs?"

"It's my lucky rock; you see it was in the war, the big one to end all wars. I don't know why I wasn't shipped with color to be one our secret weapons. They were driving those GI trucks and they needed supplies from France into Germany.

Instead, I was sent and trained with them ground pounders, our infantry. One night I'm on patrol with six white boys.

"We got caught just as I stepped on this rock and fell on my face. My whole group, six good shoulders bought their folks the ranches.

"Because I fell just before the bullets came, the krauts missed me. So I just laid still, did a little shaking, though." Them krauts left. I found my Thompson and this rock. Don't know if it was the same German patrol, I ran into earlier. "But there were six of them. So I blasted them up and down with my Thompson. "Came home after the war still untouched carrying this rock. I call it 'my lucky rock. Where to, boss?" "Drive to where the Olympic Swimming finals are being held, Dusty.

"You got tickets, Boss?" "No. I'm depending on your magic rock for two tickets." "Well, I'd better get me polishing it right now." Cooper watches and is surprised, Dusty is holding his rock, which is slightly smaller than a soccer ball, between his thighs and is steering the car with his knees. His hands are covered with a large red Western handkerchief.

Dusty is certainly giving his lucky stone a first class rub. His stone is shining.

Cooper envies Dusty's steering with his knees. Dusty sighs out, "Mr. Cooper we are here. Them seats have been sold out for a couple of months. You think you gonna get a ticket?

"Nope, Dusty. Two tickets. One for you and one for me." "But boss, they ain't got no more tickets."

"Faith, Dusty, Faith. I'm betting on your rock. Let's try it out. Cooper and Dusty walk past fifteen ticket boxes which are closed. The last box is an On Call box. A young lady is sitting inside doing her nails.

Cooper walks up to the box and says, "I'm sorry I am late but my plane had engine trouble in some out of the way airport. My uncle and I had to wait for a part not worth more than a nickel for four dry days with the 168License. My sister and that's her uncle, and he would sure like to see his niece swim today."

The ticket girl looks again above her where the "on call" tickets are kept. Only two tickets remain. She shakes her head and takes down the box with only two tickets left and holds them in her hand.

Finally she says, "Take them. They're the best seats in the house. Please don't tell anyone how you got those tickets. Would that be the blind girl that's swimming?"

"That's my sister, Sally." Cooper shows Sally's picture that he carries in his wallet.

The ticket seller tells Cooper, "God love her." And she hands Cooper the last two tickets. She drops the curtain and locks her booth.

Cooper hurries to Dusty. Thanks for the rubbing; we got our tickets and they are the best in the house, let's go."

When entering the swimming pool building where the races are, Cooper must show his tickets to an usher.

"Sorry, sir, no rocks are allowed in this building." Cooper, in almost a whisper says, "That rock is an old custom in Africa where my uncle has his diamond mines. That rock he carries is from his Number 3 mine, and he's taking it to show to your college President.

There's going to be, as I understand, a new Science building in my uncle's name. That rock goes into the corner stone.

"You know, it's just too darn expensive to stick it somewhere, and someone might walk off with it.

"This rock came by plane with Uncle Dusty carrying that priceless rock on his lap, that he loves, to keep as glossy as he can."

"Well, OK, but can he keep it between his legs so it won't roll around?"

"No problem. He understands." The clerk smiles. "You two have the best seats in the house." Jude was with Greta, Dr, Terry McGill, with Eduard Brunner, and Franziska have the only seats Jude could get by pulling his weight with the many customers he'd had.

Sitting around Jude's guests are interested people who have now heard that the blind girl's parents and friends are right next to them.

Suddenly everyone became friends after hearing about Cooper and Sally's stories as cow hand rustlers, finding the lost child, and their bicycle ride to Yosemite National Park.

Then, they hear the story about why Cooper, Sally's brother, could not attend his sister's swimming races.

Jude stands up and searches the crowd again, with his 10 power glasses.

Greta asks, "Jude, you know Cooper couldn't attend. Franziska told us why Cooper could not attend."

"I know that and I know our son. I'm going to take one more look." Jude begins to make another search. Suddenly, Jude drops to his seat.

All he said was, "I just can't believe it." He calls for Eduard. "Take these glasses and search the prime seat area right in the middle. Whom do you see?

At the same time, their new friends raise their glasses to search the area. "My word it's my future brother-in-law. Franzie, he's here sitting like the president, and dressed as if he has been thinning lettuce for a week with no change of clothes.

"Then, he seems to have with him one of the workers. How does he do these things and win?"

These people are watching with binoculars and 'zero in' on the subject of the day.

They are laughing and crying at the same time. They have already heard stories about Sally and Cooper. Some of the people that heard the stories from California accepted them hesitantly. Now, they believe the stories."

No one, even Greta and Jude, can understand how Cooper arrived here, when he said he couldn't. Then he was seated with another man. Greta claims, "This could not be Cooper. He just doesn't wear this type of clothes."

This idea was quickly confirmed by Franziska and Greta.

Then to be seated, both men, in the best seats in the house. The man next to Cooper, as Cooper appears to know him, keeps rubbing a rock with a western cowboy-type handkerchief.

Jude turns to Franziska: "What have you been feeding our son to have him dress and act like this?"

"Jude, I hadn't seen him or heard from him in six days as he was doing something in a closed off part of the school's lab.

"In fact when I saw him last, I left his secured lab in a tantrum and darn near knocked his lead instructor on the floor.

"I was so mad that I sat in my car for some time before I had the nerve to even to turn on the key to start my car. I was boiling.

"When I was coming up here with you people, I remembered my Dad had the same lead instructor at Stanford many years before. Dad, a West Pointer, was cool and never flustered, and went through similar treatment and survived with quick promotions and honors.

"I'm lost watching that strange man with Cooper that has a large rock on his lap and he keeps rubbing the darn thing.

Franziska continues, "Well, here come the girls. They have good looking racing suits. I wonder how they can wiggle in getting ready to swim."

Sally is last and is guided by a dark-haired swimmer.

Franziska mentions, "Oh, that's Edie. She's the one Sally is living with instead of living with the rest of the girls in a dorm."

Greta enters into the discussion, "According to the local papers, this caused a near revolt of the swimmers against the judges.

"There was a fight over that. I understand the girls nearly quit over some rule requiring that all must be together. Where they had Sally wasn't the safest place for a sightless person, let alone for one that can see."

Greta continues, "I was told, the other swimmers nearly walked off if Sally was forced to live in the selected dorm.

"The dark haired swimmer, next to Sally, I believe her name is Edie. "Yes. She's leading Sally. It's strange that her racing times are extremely close to Sally's times. I think her father is a doctor." Jude then describes some rules to the new friends. "Sally, being blind, has the lane next to the pool's edge. "In all of her races, a coach is allowed to walk along side Sally ready to blow a whistle; if Sally moves too close to the pool's edge or close to the lane next to her, he can blow a whistle. Then, another whistle, with a different key sound tells Sally she's ready to turn around. It's in the rules. Except, this is not valid at these races here.

"Sally can be whistled only for turns, and there's No help on the lanes. This rule was just added this week by some one. It sure stirred up a storm.

"The girl Sally is staying with, her father is on the, I guess it would be called, the racing committee. I understand he almost went through the ceiling over the change in this rule.

"They, these committee guys wanted no help for Sally even with the coach on the turns. I understand the whole racing team of girls refused to even swim if that rule stands. They packed their clothes and were walking out of this gym and refused to compete. So they changed the rules."

Incidentally the girl next to Sally, Edie, has pulled the lane next to Sally in the three races. Again the judges wanted another pull for lanes. "All the girls, especially Edie, fought that sudden new rule and won again. She's the girl Sally is living with at her home. "Finally the judges caved in again, as the swimmers threatened another walk out." Now the racers step up on each of their racing platforms. Edie helps Sally up on her platform and gets Sally's feet placed correctly before Edie climbs on her platform. The crowd cheers.

This is a 50 meter race: Up and back.

All twelve girls hit the water together. The turns are close. Slowly, the two girls, Edie and Sally merge a stroke ahead and are almost at a tie at the finish.

After a long deliberation Edie is announced as the winner by one hundredth of a second. The crowd moans. Edie turns Sally around and directs her where to wave.

This brings the crowd to their feet, cheering along with the other racers. More than a few in the audience wiped their eyes.

Two other girls with Edie get Sally situated to stand on the correct platform to receive her medal. There are more cheers.

One hour later the 100 meter race begins. When the girls come in a line, Edie is walking with Sally with the help of another girl.

Some judges tried to have the three girls stay in a straight line as they walked out from the dressing room. Sally is not walking correctly. Edie and other racer are helping Sally.

Edie keeps pointing to Sally's right side. Now Edie is talking to a Judge. He keeps shaking his head.

Jude leans over to Greta and Dr. Terri McGill. "Any idea what's going on down there, ladies?"

Dr. Terri shakes her head. "But something is wrong with Sally. That dark haired girl, the one that beat Sally in the first race knows something but isn't getting that something across to the judges. I'll watch."

Now as the girls line up behind their start platforms, three girls stand next to Sally before introductions.

A judge hurries to the girls and waves his hands. The girls with Sally shake their heads. There is some talking going on.

Suddenly the remaining girls gather around the Judge. Something is going on.

Sally's coach, appears to be ordered away from the discussion.

A tall man in a blue suit tries to enter the discussion. He's also ordered away, but not before he had something to say.

The girls return to their starting stations except Sally and Edie and another racer. They help Sally to her platform.

Sally is at a slight right lean while on the platform. The race begins for the 100 meters.

Edie and Sally are out in front at least one length ahead. The turns are together and Sally finishes one tenth of a second ahead of Edie.

Edie and the two other racers help Sally out of the pool to the 'Ready Room' in front of the girl's dressing room.

Terri tells Greta and Jude, "I'm going to see Sally. Something is not right."

An attendant refused to let Terri enter the room. Right behind Terri is a tall man in a light blue suit, who, also, is refused entrance.

As they both turn to leave, the tall man mentions, Edie is my daughter and I'm a doctor. Something is very wrong with Sally."

He looks at Terri. Are you her mother?" "No. I'm her Doctor." "Well doctor, that's my daughter, Edie. After the next race I suggest, even if we have to roll up our sleeves, we will find out what Sally's problems are."

Terri answers, "I believe it's ass kicking time." "Are you good on Ass Kicking, Doctor?"

Terri smiles. "In Trumps. See you, Doctor, right after the next race."

It wasn't a happy group of swimmers coming out for the last race. Sally and Eddie were last out and Sally is holding her right side and Edie is pointing toward a bleacher area then to Sally's right side.

These girls came out as bunch appearing to disregard the Marshall's urging to be in a line. Instead of standing at their start platforms, the swimmers bunched around Sally and Edie.

The P A announcer isn't getting the girls lined up. One male Marshall made a bad mistake. He tried to push a swimmer toward her starting platform.

He was grabbed by three swimmers who showed him to the pool. It was apparent, that with one more of his dumb moves, he'd be in the water. The crowd cheered.

Finally, the racers wandered to their stations except Sally,. Edie, and another racer. They are still standing and talking to three judges.

Sally's coach, with the whistle, tries to enter into this discussion and was ordered back to his station.

Finally the talking ended. Edie has been moved to one more lane over from Sally. Why? No one knows. There are murmurs in the crowd.

Again the two girls help Sally up onto her platform. Sally has a further lean now than in the previous race.

Between Edie, one more lane over, and the racer next to Sally are still talking to Sally who keeps shaking her head.

The announcer threatens to have this race stopped unless the girl racers stop talking.

Suddenly all racers including Sally and Edie walk away from their racing blocks. This indicates a problem.

There follows more discussions with judges and racers. Finally Edie is changed back to her position next to Sally.

The spectators in the packed gym cheer. Then the other racers return to their blocks.

Edie is helping Sally position her feet on her racing block.

Edie looks toward an certain spectator area and places her right hand below her ribs and nods her head.

A judge rushes over to Edie and is telling her something using a loud voice and shaking his finger at her.

He's telling her something when ten women racers, again step off their starting blocks.

A sudden scream comes from the audience. Sally has collapsed and has fallen into the pool.

Two spectators almost flew out of their seats. Cooper was followed by Eduard. Some man tried to stop the athletic 220 pound Eduard. Well, he received an unassisted slam into the pool by Eduard.

Dr. Terri has reached the pool at the same time the blue suit jumps in the pool and helps the others. Three men are holding Sally.

Jude arrives after pushing two men in suits into the pool. He joins up with his daughter, Edie, Cooper and Eduard and the man in the blue suit. Sally is breathing but is unconscious.

The man in the blue suit yells out, "I want an ambulance right now." He is informed the ambulance has left to handle a serious wreck. Cooper hollers out: "Dusty, get your car to the main entrance now bring your stone with you.

A stretcher is brought to the pools' edge. Sally, now unconscious, is loaded on. Jude gave his daughter a kiss.

Now Jude, Eduard and Cooper carry Sally to the outside door that suddenly opens.

Dusty tells Cooper, "Doors open, we're ready to go." Sally is on the back seat on the stretcher. The man in the blue suit and Terri are with Sally. Cooper and Eduard crowded into the front giving Dusty room to drive.

Dusty asks Cooper, "Where to, boss?" The doctor in the blue suit replies. "Sixth and Opel and hurry." Dusty replies, "Got it." Away they go. The Doctor asks Cooper, "Do you trust this driver?" Dusty gives Cooper a side ways look. Cooper replies, "With every thing I own." It wasn't long when Dusty announces, "We are here." The doctor tells Cooper, "I want to talk to your driver. Don't let him leave, please."

# CHAPTER 16

THERE WAS A WAIT before the gurney was rolled up to Sally. Then she disappears inside the emergency entrance.

The man in the blue suit stays. "Don't worry.

I have a minute to spare. "They have to get the emergency equipment up and going. I am Doctor De La Croix, Edie's father.

I have been doing, what I think Sally has, for twenty years. She now has Peritonitis from a ruptured appendix.

First things first. You must be Cooper, Sally's brother. And this guy next to you must be Eduard. As I understand, you, Eduard, are engaged to Sally?"

Are you two boys available to spend two or more weeks with Sally while she's unconscious? I'll have a medical team with her all the time.

Almost in one voice came, "We will." "OK. I'll have a nurse fix you two with white shoes, pants, a shirt and an ID to hang on your neck. Cooper, your clothes you have no use in keeping.

After Sally's operation, I'll meet with you two again and the families. "Dr. McGill, I have clothes and an ID for you along with a view of the operation coming up. Cooper, where's your excellent driver?

Cooper points over to Dusty, who is rubbing his rock with a western handkerchief with gusto. Dr. De La Croix asks Cooper what your driver is doing now?

Cooper replies, "That's his lucky stone and it works." "Hmmm. I'll let him keep it. We will need all the luck we can get."

Cooper speaks up. "I think it works." Now the family arrives. Cooper and Eduard have shaved, showered and are wearing white clothes. Sitting next to the wide door to the Emergency area is Dusty dressed in white coveralls. He's in leaning against an ambulance rubbing his rock.

He hollers to Cooper. "Hey, boss, Thank you. You got me a good job. I'm rubbing my rock for your sister. Don't worry, boss. Now, you know it works.

Franziska asks, Honey, what's this about that rock? I saw him rubbing the rock constantly during the races."

"I'll tell you later. This you won't believe." "Yeah. I'm going to marry a man that has strange friends, an extremely odd professor, and my future husband isn't telling how he got here. Were you shot out of a cannon?"

"Very close, very close. That's another story, later." "OK. What about your damnable project that nearly separated us. I'm still mad."

"I have nothing to say right now. But this. I won the ball game." That's a period. Not until Sally is ready to travel will I return to Poly and see the results. I'm not worried until I begin teach Eduard how to surf."

Franziska grabs Cooper and kisses him. "I'm really really sorry I acted like a bitch. Will you accept my apologies?"

"Maybe on or after our seventh wedding anniversary, I might." The families wait 'til Sally is taken to a room. She is unconscious.

Dr. De La Croix will meet with the Portages and families.

Dr. Terri joins the family as they wait for the doctor.

Dr. Terri outlines her views. "Dr. De Lacroix is an artist. One problem is that Sally's appendix isn't where the book tells us it should be.

Dr. De La Croix went at it as if he knew where Sally's appendix was. There were no problems. He told me he has handled the appendix and peritonitis for twenty years without a patient lost. This is a very touchy operation. Problems can develop quickly.

"He was ready as he just knew, earlier what he was going to find. Three interns watch the pro. They were as impressed as I was.

"It was a very smooth operation. It has been years and years since I've been this situation. But, this man is fantastic.

"When he cleans up and rechecks Sally he will meet with all of us.

An hour or so later Sally is wheeled unconscious to her room. Dr. De La Croix now explains: Sally will be unconscious for about, at least two weeks. Notice the tubes she has in her abdomen. We have to keep draining her.

I have one nurse and one intern on duty for two and a half hour shifts; that's twenty four hours a day. They are watching the drainage, pressure, heart beat and a lot more.

"Sometimes a drainage tube or two will plug up. Then we have to hurry back to that room."

"Or maybe blood pressure or pulse or something will plug up. Then, we go down the hallway to surgery again for unplugging.

"Blood pressure, breathing, heart beat and more is watched 24 hours a day. I have been doing this for 23 years and have never lost a patient. Oh sure, we've had some tight moments.

I will not attend the olympics this year even with my daughter, who is competing. Edie understands my medical philosophy.

"A patient remains a patient long after your patient goes home. My interns and the nurses know this rule of mine, completely.

Both intern and nurse nodded their heads and smiled.

Now the two lads, Cooper and Eduard. First: I had Sally for some days, in our house before the event. It was my daughter, Edie that fought the battle to bring Sally to our house. Let me say this, I have a true daughter then I have Sally who is blind. I'm thinking our house will tone down.

"No way. I must say to the Portages and Dr. McGill, you young people have done a training and raising; I've never seen any child face a life in the dark like Sally.

Then the two, what do I say, her brother and man she was going to marry after the Olympics. I thought these two boys, pardon me, these young men, according to Sally, there's not another male human being that can compare with these two unbelievable young men. And what's great, you two guys are almost twin brothers.

Eduard, do you know how far you threw that swimming judge? It was the best toss I've seen. It sure served that stuffy bunch correctly.

These set of judges operated incorrectly during the start of practice to the finals. This will be on our agenda at our next meeting along with the film shots.

"I'm glad and proud to have such good lads do their part for the next two or more weeks."

# CHAPTER 17

On the third day the head nurse grabs Eduard and Cooper, as they are exchanging shifts. "OK, boys, There are three florist trucks chock full of flowers in front of our hospital. They might fit in our auditorium, but not in Sally's room. What are your thoughts?"

Both lads spoke up together. "Wait a minute, one at a time, please. Brother or future husband.

Take a pick.

Eduard speaks up. "I'm speaking for the family as, I didn't have a chance to tell you, Coop, I just passed the bar test to be a lawyer. So I'm legally representing the family."

Cooper clips in, "Here comes his first law money." Eduard suggests. "I'm really speaking for Cooper and myself. Give us all the cards. As we spend time with Sally, we'll write thank you notes.

"Coop, I'm speaking for you, too. There must be sick people in this hospital who have not received one flower.

"Can you divide these flowers to give out to patients without flowers? I'm sure you can think of some suitable words when you hand around flowers they would never have received.

"If there are any more flowers showing up later, then, do the same." Sara, the Head Nurse wipes her eyes. "I've been on his race course for 35 years. This is the first time, fellows, the first time this has ever happened. Damn you, guys, I'm getting tears in my eyes just thinking of the good you two have just done. Thank you, again."

In the second week Sally is showing some movements. She has been talking about her needs, for a bath and such.

Eduard asks Cooper, "Let's grab some coffee or tea at the restaurant on the first floor. I want to talk to you alone." Eduard smiles.

"Let's go in the restaurant's back corner. "First, Franziska has just received her transfer to Poly this year to finish her major. She has a tentative position in a school district.

Now you. You had a note in your letter, but she couldn't take it. So she talked to your old Prof, Dr. Fredor Sokolov.

He's leaving the college; retiring is the word. Hang on. He has suggested for you to take his job at school. Your school has accepted you on a trial basis.

He has given your name into whatever that scientific group that handles Doctoral honors."

"Are you still with me, Coop?" Eduard notices tears in Cooper's eyes. "He also left some papers to sign and keys for you. Do you know where the keys fit?" "Not on Santa Catalina Island, remarks Cooper. "Yep."

Eduard reaches in his pocket and hands the keys to Cooper. Cooper is in tears.

Eduard hands Cooper his own handkerchief. "Well, buddy, you earned it." Cooper, red eyed, looks at Eduard. I'm not going to accept those keys." "Coop, you loved that island and talked many times of having a house there, except it's very expensive. I heard you say that many time when we had the girls with us."

"OK, only it's you and I, and our girls. we'll partner the house. This will captivate Sally. She loved that island especially when we four were able to slip away. "Is that all the news? I hope. I hate crying on happy things. What's new with you now that you will be working in the San Luis Obispo county law offices?"

"Well, when leave here I have some days free. Why? I have no idea. But I've been looking at certain magazines. I'm going to buy a board and have my brother-in-law teach me surfing."

Another week has passed. Sally is sitting up and her days here are decreasing. Right now Jude has invited Colonel Zimmerman and his wife, Eduard's mother and father, along with Terry for a weekend.

Cooper is talking to Eduard. There's one thing about Sally I can't figure out. I think she reads minds, as she can read my mind.

I haven't said a word to Sally about Santa Catalina. We have been there a few times.

"So why don't we take the girls, when Sally is able, for a weekend on the island in our new rest house.

"Well, Coop, let's show ourselves to the families. Before reaching Sally's room, they can hear Sally talking. "Yes. It will be six couples and Terri to spend few days on Catalina Island, so we can be better acquainted. I'm sure we can get the key. "Coop, Eduard, Dad, where did our boys go? Did I just see those two guys walk right past my room without stopping?" Cooper has his arm around Eduard's neck. "Who gets to kick who first!"